When Havyn pretends to be her best friend on a date with the mafia Don in her city in Italy, she doesn't expect to fall in love with him.

Alessandro has always been known as cold-hearted, but the moment he lays eyes on Havyn, something in him shifts, and he finds himself falling, too.

Amore Mio
Copyright © 2024 Wie-aam Adams
ISBN: 978-1-4874-4112-8
Cover art by Martine Jardin

Published by eXtasy Books Inc

Look for us online at:
www.eXtasybooks.com

Amore Mio
The Romano Brothers

By

Wie-aam Adams

CHAPTER ONE: HAVYN

"No."

Adia rolls her eyes at my defiance, sifting through her closet of clothes.

"Why? It's just one date," she grumbles.

"Yeah, just one date with the head of the Italian mafia," I say, reminding her. The thought that she might have forgotten that tiny little detail crosses my mind. The mere thought of being in the same room as someone as dangerous as that makes my skin crawl, never mind having to sit through an entire dinner with him, which Adia begs me to do.

"So what?" she questions, turning to me with an expression that tells me she doesn't understand why I'm having such a hard time agreeing to this. "It's just one date, Havyn. You'll get to dine with expensive food and wine for free for the first time in your life. And I didn't want to use this, but . . . the guy's really hot." She squeals at the end of her sentence, her face scrunching up in excitement.

"If he's so hot, then why aren't you going on a date with him? Why send me in your place instead?" I question, crossing my arms across my chest.

"You know why," she insists, glaring down at me from where she stands. "I've been told that he's very inquisitive and smart. The moment I step into that restaurant, my cover will get blown."

I hate to admit it, but she's right. Someone like him pays attention to every single detail, every single action, every single word. And when Adia lays her eyes on an attractive woman, it's over for the both of us. Her father will, well, ground her, only because she's his daughter, but me? He'll probably have me shipped off to one of those poor villages where I have to farm vegetables for the rest of my life.

"Havyn," she whispers, coming forward to grab my hands. "You know how much keeping this secret means to me. If that mafia Don finds out and tells my father, I'll be locked up in this place for the rest of my life."

I try not to look into her eyes, especially when I catch a glimpse of those puppy eyes of hers. It's my weakness, honestly, but only when it comes to her, anyway. I pull my hands out of hers, looking away from her.

"Why don't you just pretend to be interested in this guy?" I suggest, her eyebrows furrowing at my words. "I mean, think about it. I heard that the heads of the mafias aren't exactly loyal men, so he can get himself mistresses while you have your own . . . mistresses, too."

"You really think it's possible to hide such a thing from a man like him?" She scoffs, crossing her arms. "You don't know that man. Nothing goes past him."

"Well, then, I'm out of ideas!" I exclaim, plopping onto the edge of her bed. She follows, sitting down next to me much more gracefully than I just did.

"Havyn, everything will be solved if you just go on that one date with him," she insists.

"And what if he wants to proceed with the marriage after that?" I question.

"He won't," she says, a certain surety in her voice.

"How do you know that?" I ask, narrowing my eyes at her.

"Look, it's no secret that he doesn't want to get married. He's only agreed to this date because it's what his father wants," she says, and I nod against my better judgment. "Besides, I . . . you aren't the only woman he'll be going on a date with."

"I'm not?" I exclaim in surprise. She shakes her head.

"Nope. He's going on multiple dates with multiple women to see which one he likes the most," she explains.

"So basically, the chances of him choosing you . . . me are slim," I say, and she nods.

"Exactly."

That does put me at ease, if I'm honest. But still, I'm not doing it.

"Havyn!" Adia whines, pulling at my arm with her fingers. "Just this once. It'll be the last time, I promise."

I close my eyes. "Let's weigh the pros and cons."

Cons — He's dangerous.

He may kill me at the end of the date.

He might, for some odd reason, choose me as his bride.

Pros — Adia will get to keep her secret.

Adia will be happy.

I open my eyes. The cons are more than the pros, but just as I'm about to tell Adia no for the final time, her puppy eyes appear before me, and I find my resolve slipping. She's doing this on purpose. She knows I can't say no to her puppy eyes. This sneaky little —

"And? Have you made your decision?" she pipes out, cutting through my train of thought. I sigh in defeat.

"Fine. I'll do it."

I barely have a second to grasp what just came out of my own mouth before Adia launches herself at me, wrapping her long arms around my tiny frame and pushing us both down onto the bed.

"You're the best," she exclaims, placing kisses all over my face. "I love you. I love you. I love you."

"Okay, that's enough," I say, pushing her away. For a single moment, I see a small pout on her lips before it morphs into a wide smile.

"You won't regret this. I'm forever indebted to you," she says, placing a hand on her chest.

3

I try not to roll my eyes at her words. I'm pretty sure I'll regret saying yes the moment I walk into the date with no chance to run away.

"Just pray that I'm still alive at the end of it," I mutter, and she laughs in response. Although, I'm not joking.

"You're worrying for nothing, Havyn. I'm sure it'll be over before you even get to say the word pray," she assures, patting my shoulder. I frown at her, shrugging her hand off. She has no idea what she just talked me into. I don't even know what I just got talked into.

All I can do is hope that whoever this man is, he won't decide to slit my throat as an afterparty.

CHAPTER TWO: HAVYN

"It's too tight."

Adia rolls her eyes at me, tugging at the string, causing me to suck in a breath.

"Maybe if you'd stop moving and wiggling your body, this would already have been over," she snaps.

"Do we really need to do a fitting and have a dress made for this date?" I choke out, pursing my lips at the tightness of the string she has wrapped around my body. Is this how Snow White felt?

"Of course. He thinks he's going to be dining with the finest Adia Hamilton. If you're going to pretend to be me successfully, you have to dress the part," she says, and I scoff.

"I'm sorry. Who's doing who a favour here?" I retort. Adia doesn't answer. I thought so.

"Just give me a second. I'm almost done taking your measurements," she says.

"Who's even going to be making the dress? None of your tailors will be able to make it without your father finding out," I say.

"He won't find out. Just trust me," she says, dismissively.

"It's hard to when you can easily cut off my circulation with one single movement," I say.

"I don't appreciate your sass, miss," she snaps, tugging at the string as if to teach me a lesson to watch my words. I gasp in surprise.

"You know why I'm being like this," I mumble, fidgeting with the sleeves of my shirt, and she sighs. She knows.

Whenever I'm nervous or anxious about something, I tend to be sassy about everything. It's my attempt at distracting myself from the impending problem. It does work, but only up until a certain point, and then I usually just crash down in tears. I'm hoping to skip that stage this time.

"I'm sorry," Adia mumbles, looking down in shame.

I don't respond, merely keeping my eyes away from her as she finally releases me from the string, and I gasp for breath.

"The date is tomorrow night. Your dress will be ready by the morning."

"Adia," I call out, reaching out to grab her arm. "I know you didn't mean anything by it. I'm just nervous, and it's making me extra sensitive. That's all."

She nods, her lips tugging upwards into a smile. She leans down, pulling me into a hug. "Thank you, and I'm sorry."

I laugh.

I hope I can still laugh at the end of tomorrow night.

CHAPTER THREE: HAVYN

"It's cold."

I tighten the binds of my puffer jacket, trying to prevent as much cold air from entering the little open spaces as possible. I hold my arm up, noting that it's almost midnight on my wristwatch. It's probably not ideal for me to be walking outside all alone at this hour, seeing as there could be literally any predators lurking in the shadows, just waiting for the right moment to strike. But then again, it's not like I had any choice. It's not like I could have spent the night at Adia's house.

Technically, Adia and I keep our friendship a secret, meaning that I can only be at her home when her father's out working. Her father doesn't quite like me, and that's putting it lightly. He practically spits on the ground that I walk on, and truly, there's only one simple reason why.

I don't have money. Unlike all of their acquaintances, I'm not filthy rich. Instead, I'm an orphan, adopted by a problematic couple who ultimately left me with emotional scars that haven't healed in years. I honestly don't think they will ever heal. They'll just remain a part of me, until the day I finally leave this world.

Adia's father will have a fit if he sees the kind of place I live in. He would probably have me beaten up, or even worse, especially if he finds out about Adia's and my secret friendship.

With a sigh, I come to a stop right in front of my rundown apartment complex in the slums. I bet those rich people still think this place is a myth, but it can't be more real. And I live in it.

With a heavy heart, I continue walking, trying to step over all the shattered beer bottles and cigarettes before I finally find myself on the stairs. The staircase isn't any better, stained yellow with urine and black from cigarette ash. I even see a splotch of blood on the wall as I make my way up.

Others may freak out if they see the state of this place, but I'm used to it. It's not like my life was any better with my adopted parents. I used to dream about getting adopted by a kind young couple who would love me in the way my biological parents never did, but all I got was a weak father and an overly aggressive mother. Not a very good mix.

My apartment door isn't locked and slightly ajar when I reach it. Don't tell me they did drugs in my apartment again. I don't even have to take a step into the apartment before the smell of cannabis invades my nostrils. I bite my lower lip in anger, slamming the door shut before stomping over to the end of the hall to the landlord's door.

Clenching my hand into a fist, I pound on the door, shouting, "Open up, Randy!"

The door opens after a few more knocks, revealing a not-surprising high Randy. Randy is a 40-year-old drunk with a balding head and a beer belly that he can't tuck into his pants no matter how hard he tries. He's also the owner of this building, my landlord.

"What do you want, Miller?" he questions, taking a jug of the vodka bottle he holds in his one hand.

"I remember telling you that my apartment is off-limits," I growl.

"And I remember telling you that this is my building, and I can do whatever the hell I want," he says, gesturing forward with the vodka bottle. I roll my eyes at him.

"And then I gave you extra cash so that you would give the key to my apartment to me," I say.

"Turns out I had another spare." He shrugs, feigning ignorance. "Oops."

"Give it to me," I say, holding my hand out to him.

"And if I don't?" he taunts, tilting his head at me.

"You know me, Randy. I don't take anyone's bullshit," I practically growl, glaring him down. For a few long moments, he doesn't say anything, and when a sinister smirk appears on his face, I know that it can't be any good. *What does he have up his sleeve now?*

"You know, I recall reviewing your lease agreement a couple of days ago and noticed that it expires soon," he drawls, his yellow-stained teeth making their appearance.

No.

"You can't kick me out," I snap, panic creeping into my nerves. "I've lived here for two years now. You know me, Randy!"

"Oh, I do. I do," he carelessly mutters, as if to turn what I just said into nothing. "And that's why I'm forced to ask you to move out. I've gotten bored of your attitude, you see."

"You can't do this," I exclaim.

"Oh, but I can," he retorts, taking another gulp of his vodka. "You have two days to get out, and if you insist on staying, I'll have my dogs throw you out."

He's not bluffing. I've seen the guys he hangs out with. Tall, muscular guys who can tear me in half with their bare hands.

"And it won't be pretty if I send them," he drawls, his fingers coming up to trail down my jawline. "I wouldn't want to ruin this pretty face. It's all you got."

I swat his hand away, sending him one last fierce glare before stomping off to my apartment and slamming the door closed behind me.

That bastard. He knew this would happen. That's why no matter how much money I gave him, he still came back and did nasty things in my apartment. He knew I had nowhere to go and was just waiting for my contract to expire to kick me out. I admit, to him and his associates, I'm not the nicest person, but I didn't think that my defiance and strong nature would drive them to hate me.

I still remember when I first moved in at the ripe age of sixteen. I was young and in my prime, so he took me in, and called me the prettiest thing he'd ever laid his eyes on. He called me his favourite, and I guess I was before I saw my first rape take place before my very eyes. Randy held me close to him, forcing me to keep my eyes on the scene as a man, one of his friends, did terrible things to an innocent girl.

That was the day I decided to change. I decided that if I didn't become tough, one day, that girl would be me, and the more I changed, the less Randy liked me, and now, I guess he's finally fed up with me.

Of course, I'm still the old me with people whom I've known for years, which is only Adia, but still. I allow myself to be vulnerable and even weak around her because I trust her and know that she will never put me in a compromising position. Well, I guess that was until she convinced me to go on a date with the Italian mafia Don in her stead.

I'm still not too sure how I feel about that, but one thing's for sure — I'm terrified. With Randy, I can still handle him, but this . . . this is different. This is the mafia we're talking about. He's way more powerful than Randy. In fact, he puts Randy's *gang* to shame.

The date is less than 24 hours away, and I still have no idea what the guy's name is or what he looks like. A person would think that people would talk about such a powerful man, but they don't. If anything, it's like they've been sworn to silence. And this leaves me with no choice but to just rely on whatever Adia says, which isn't much besides how powerful and hot he is. If I didn't know her so well, I'd think she was actually into men.

With a heavy sigh, I collapse onto the couch, wincing when my bottom hits hard wood. I try to hold in my frustration. The cotton has been ripped, and all stuffing has long disappeared with no trace. I can't even get comfortable in my own home. I get up and walk to my bedroom, not bothering to lock the door since Randy has a key and will come in when he wants, whether I lock it or not.

I don't bother stripping out of my clothes. I fall onto my bed, the only remotely comfortable piece of furniture in my apartment, not that I have anything besides a bed, couch, and dressing table with a mirror with a long diagonal crack.

With one last sigh, I let sleep consume me.

Chapter Four: Havyn

Tonight is the night.
The date.

I'm freaking out.

"Calm down. It'll all go well. I'm sure," Adia assures, stabbing yet another bobby pin into my scalp.

I moved out this morning, but I didn't tell Adia. No, it's rather that I couldn't because the moment I walked through those estate gates, she had me up in her room for make-up, hair, and the *works*. Also, I don't want to burden her with my problems. She does enough for me as it is. And it's not like she has anything to be suspicious about when I'm acting the same way I usually do, and even though I packed everything I own this morning, it all fits into my backpack since I don't own much, and I always carry my backpack around with me, so nothing is out of place or different.

Now, as the clock strikes 7 PM, Adia's doing the last touches to my hair. I haven't seen myself since this morning. When I had to put the dress on, Adia blindfolded me with a scarf and literally dressed me herself just because she wanted me to see myself with the entire look completed. Even now, she has me facing away from the mirror, glaring at me when I try to take a sneak peek at myself every moment she looks away.

"Adia, you haven't exactly told me what tonight consists of. All you've said so far is that it's a formal date. But where? Not his place, right? Because if so, he could kill me and get rid of my body without anyone knowing . . ."

Adia shushes me by shoving a marshmallow into my mouth. I scrunch my face up in distaste. She's been munching on these all day, and she knows I hate the taste of them.

"Stop overthinking this. It's not such a big deal," she says dismissively, causing me to wince when she simultaneously pulls on a strand of hair too hard.

"Not a big deal?" I scoff, glaring up at her, but she can hardly be bothered. "I'm dining with the Italian mafia Don. What about that doesn't scream big deal?"

"Look," she says, leaning down slightly to look into my eyes. "All you have to do tonight is to be present and go with the flow. Do whatever he tells you to, and don't argue."

Don't argue. She knows that's one of my struggles with new and strange people. And just do whatever he tells me to? I'm not a loyal dog that he can just order around.

"So, the date will be taking place at a party. It's more of a fancy ball with slow dancing than a party, but yeah. You'll be his date at this ball," she explains.

"But how will I be able to find him? I don't even know what he looks like," I exclaim.

"I sent him a picture of the dress you'll be wearing. He'll look for you in that dress," she says.

"Can I at least know his name?" I slightly plead, wanting to know just about anything about this man. I can't go into the date not knowing anything at all. That's like emotional suicide, maybe physical, as well.

"Alessandro Romano is his name. And if you really want to find him before he finds you, just look for the sexiest man in the room, and that's him," she says with a chuckle.

"Are you sure you're not secretly into men?" I question, narrowing my eyes at her. She merely rolls her eyes at me in response. She does a few more touch-ups to my appearance, and finally, after what feels like forever, she lets go of me and takes a step back.

"You're finished," she exclaims, clasping her hands together with a proud smile on her face. I don't waste a second getting up from the chair and turning to the mirror. What I see makes me gasp.

I've always been pretty, or at least that's what others have told me, but this . . . this is different. I dare say I look gorgeous. Make-up really does bring out every single glow and perfection in a person. Here I stand in the most beautiful dress I have ever seen. It's a ballgown that flairs up at my waist, with sparkly details travelling down from my bust to the hem and drop sleeves. The flowy material of the gown from the waist down is a beautiful dusty pink colour. A silver necklace with a single diamond, the same colour as the dress, hangs around my neck, a crystal-like bracelet wrapped around my wrist, and a simple silver ring with a rose gold pearl on it sits on my right hand's ring finger. My hair is flowing down my back in curls with a few strands pinned to the back and my baby hairs framing my face. For make-up, thankfully, she went for minimalism with just lip gloss, dusty pink blush, and bright pink liquid eyeshadow.

If this look had one theme, I know what it would be. Innocence.

I look like a literal virgin princess. At least one of those things is true, while the other . . . not so much. If anything, Adia's the princess between the two of us.

"What do you think?" Adia asks, pulling me out of my thoughts. "I know that you don't like all the fancy make-up, so I tried to tone it down as much as I could."

I turn around to face Adia and smile. "I love it."

A big smile blooms on her face, and she excitedly nods before walking to her bed and opening the shoebox that lies on it. She beckons me to come over, and I do, sitting down on the edge of the bed. Adia takes a pair of silver heels out of the box and places them on the ground in front of my slipper-clad feet. Without her having to say a word, I kick the slippers off my feet and slip into the silver heels that somehow fit me perfectly.

She holds her hand out to me, and I take it, allowing her to help me onto my feet. The moment I'm up from the bed, my legs wobble slightly as I'm quite unaccustomed to wearing heels. I can already imagine how much pain my feet will be in at the end of tonight. But there's no turning back now.

"You look gorgeous, Havyn," Adia sincerely says, smiling down at me with crinkling eyes. And then her head snaps up to the clock hanging on her bedroom wall, her eyes widening. "You're going to be late!"

Barely giving me a chance to think of a response to her sudden panic, Adia grabs my hand and a silver clutch bag from the dressing table and pulls me out of the bedroom and down the long staircase to the front door. The first thing I notice when arriving outside is the sleek black *Mercedes* parked out front.

"Get in," Adia says, ushering me into the car. "Good luck."

And then the door closes.

Chapter Five: Havyn

M y heart races in my chest.

The car pulls up to possibly the biggest building I have ever seen in my entire life. It doesn't take more than a second for me to realise that we've stopped in front of a hotel, but not just any hotel, *the* hotel. The biggest and most well-known hotel in the city, owned by who exactly? The mafia Don I'm supposed to be on a date with tonight.

The name *Romano Towers* stares down at me in all its glory from the very top of the building. Romano . . . Alessandro Romano. Merely thinking about that name and who it belongs to sends shivers down my spine. I suddenly can't even remember why I agreed to go on this date in the first place. But this . . . this place, being here is dangerous. If he owns it, that means he can do whatever he wants without care, including hurting and possibly murdering me in cold blood.

"We're here, miss," the driver suddenly announces, staring at me through the mirror. I nod, swallowing heavily. The car door is opened by one of the hotel's staff members in a butler suit. Lifting up my dress slightly, I step out of the car.

The first thing I see is a fountain at the front of the building. Of course there's a fountain. How cliché.

"Name, miss?" the butler asks.

"Ha-Adia Hamilton," I say, clearing my throat. I almost gave myself away.

He nods before gesturing for me to follow him. He must have been told about Adia, well, me, I guess. The moment we enter the hotel, I'm overwhelmed by all the gold and marble features and furniture. Is that real gold? The first thing I see is a golden chandelier hanging from the ceiling and golden elevator doors sliding open and closed.

"This way, Miss. Hamilton," the butler says and leads me across what appears to be a lounge area. The deeper we walk into the hotel, the more gold I see. And if the man I'm supposed to be meeting for a date tonight owns all of this . . . I hate to admit that I know why so many rich fathers want to marry their daughters off to him. How much does all of this even cost? One night here must be like at least a couple of times my monthly rent. Where do people . . . where does *he* get all this money?

Maybe I should try selling drugs and doing all that illegal stuff he does.

The mere thought makes me want to laugh. Why would anyone come to me when they have him?

"Miss. Hamilton," the butler says, pulling me out of my thoughts. "We have arrived."

He then proceeds to grab the golden handles of the two large wooden double doors and push forward, revealing a large ballroom of sorts. There are tons of people in the room already, all conversing with one another with a glass in hand.

"You may go in now," he says, gesturing me to go inside. I do, hesitantly, and the moment I'm inside, the door immediately closes behind me, startling me slightly. The people in the room with me barely notice me. It's like I'm invisible to them.

Swallowing, I head straight for the buffet, ready to stuff my face with delicious and expensive food as payment for even coming here tonight. However, the moment I reach the buffet and look at all the finger food, my nose scrunches up in disgust. What is all of this?

Where's the cheeseburgers and fries? Where are all the calories I so love to add on?

But I guess I expected too much. This is, after all, a fancy party, so there will be foods like oysters and caviar.

Turning my body slightly, I bring my attention to all the people in the room. It doesn't take more than one single glance at them to be able to tell how influential they are. All these people in here . . . they're all very powerful people who can no doubt get away with murder. So the question is — what am I doing in a place, at a party, like this?

It doesn't take a genius to deduct that I don't belong here. Not even my dress and expensive accessories can mask where I'm truly from. The slums. I don't even want to think about that right now. I want . . . no, I need to live in this moment and do my best not to bring shame to the Hamilton name, but my circumstances make it difficult.

Where do I even go after this party? I was kicked out, and going back to Adia's home isn't an option. Why does life have to be so difficult?

A groan escapes me, and I have to stop myself from running my fingers through my hair and messing the hairdo up. I can't do that, not when I went through so much pain to look like this.

"And what's a pretty thing like you doing all alone?" a voice purrs, pulling me out of my thoughts. My head snaps to the source of the voice, my face instantly scrunching up in disgust. Next to me stands a middle-aged man with a balding head, a pot belly, and a blinding smile on his face. He's a short little man, his height barely matching mine, and I'm not even tall.

"I'm with someone," I say, turning my head away from him and scanning my eyes across the room. *Look for the sexiest man in the room,* Adia had said. The hottest man . . . Alessandro Romano, where are you?

"Don't lie to me, sweetheart," the man says, inching closer to me. "What man would leave such a pretty date as you all alone? Especially with all these greedy men here?"

"You mean like yourself?" I can't help but snap. The smile slips from his face.

"I do not appreciate that tone, girl," he snaps, startling me by suddenly grasping my chin in between his thick fingers. My eyes widen in alarm. "If you were invited here, then you know how powerful I must be. So I wouldn't take chances if I were you. It's not a smart move to make."

"Let go of me," I snap, swatting his hand away. His eyes darken.

"What makes you this bold, huh?" He exclaims it so loudly that it captures the attention of everyone in the room. I gulp under all their stares. "Who are you here with that you think you can just talk back to me?"

I have nothing to say. I can mention Alessandro, who I have no doubt is more powerful than this man, but I doubt he would like me bringing his name into this mess.

The man scoffs, an obnoxious smile spreading across his face. "Thought so. Now, come here and let me teach you a lesson."

My eyes widen in horror, but I'm frozen as his hand wraps around my wrist, and he tugs me forward. No one does anything to stop him, even when he stares at me with a look in his eyes that tells me he wants to devour me right in front of all these people. They all just stare. What's wrong with these people?

"Now —" he starts but breaks off amidst his sentence, his eyes widening. Almost immediately, I feel a presence behind me, and then suddenly, an arm wraps itself around my waist, and I'm pulled back, back into a hard, yet warm chest. My heart stops, my eyes wide.

What's happening? Who's this man now?

I want to look up and see who it is that's grabbed me, but my entire body is frozen. I can't move a limb.

"What do you think you're doing at my party?" the man behind me speaks, his voice sending a shudder through my entire body. His voice . . . it's so manly, with an undertone of an accent. Italian, I think.

"I'm sorry," the little man stutters out, his eyes falling to the ground. "It's just . . . she disrespected me, and I just wanted to teach her a lesson. That's all."

"And you realise that by doing this at my party, you too have disrespected me now?" the man questions.

The other man's eyes widen, his face flushing crimson. "I'm so sorry," he mutters, his face panic-stricken. "Please forgive me."

He falls to his knees.

"What do you think about this, *amore mio*?" he whispers into my ear.

Amore mio? Me? I get to have a say in this?

I swallow a lump that's formed and lodged itself in my throat. I can't speak, and sweat is trickling down my forehead.

"What would be the perfect punishment for someone who dared lay their hands on someone who belongs to me be?" he whispers.

My heart stutters in my chest. Punishment? Someone who belongs to him? Does he mean me?

"She . . . she's here with you?" the little man stutters out, sweat trickling down his balding head.

"Yes, and you made a big mistake by touching her," the man behind me says, his voice dropping an octave.

I gulp, nerves fluttering in my chest. Who is this man? Why does he hold so much power here? Why does he talk of me like I'm something he owns? And where in the world is Alessandro? Don't tell me he's just sitting back and watching this entire thing unfold.

"*Amore mio*," he softly calls out. "Have you made your decision yet?"

I gulp. Decision? How can I possibly make a decision? How did I even get myself into this position?

And then suddenly, I'm being spun around, my eyes

meeting a pair of deep green ones. My eyes widen in shock. The sexiest man in the room . . . he's standing right in front of me. The realisation hits me. This man. It's him. The one I've been thinking about this entire time. The one I fear but have been desperately seeking to come and help me.

Alessandro Romano.

Chapter Six: Havyn

Alessandro Romano is a beautiful man.

So beautiful that for a single long moment, I can't see anything but him. If there was ever a prime example of perfection, it would be him. His hair is the darkest shade of black I've ever seen and so thick and silky that I can only imagine how it must feel to run my fingers through those tresses. And then his eyes. His eyes are the deepest shade of green I've ever seen, so dark yet so transparent that I can see myself in them. However, they're almost completely hidden by his inked hair that falls onto them in the most effortless way ever. His lips . . . those cherry red plump lips that any girl without lip fillers would be envious of.

And all I can think is — how can one person be this perfect?

His eyes are on me, and his hands, his big, veiny hands, are gripping my hips so tightly that it feels as though he wants to claim me right now. Alessandro is very tall, so I have to crane my neck in order to look into his eyes. I want to look away, the look in his own eyes is too intense for me to handle, but then they flash with warning. He's telling me he doesn't want me looking away. So I don't, despite feeling as though I may be reduced to a puddle on the floor if I match his gaze for a single second longer.

"I asked how you want me to punish him," he speaks, his voice sending a shiver down my spine. Adia was right. He's sexy . . . so sexy that I've been reduced to a speechless, wide-eyed ice block.

"However you want," I finally manage to say. However,

the croakiness of my voice makes me cringe as soon as the words leave my mouth. What in the world is wrong with me? I'm Havyn. Havyn Miller. I'm no weak girl who gets influenced by sexy guys. So what the hell is happening to me right now? Oh no, is this what people call love at first sight?

No way. This has to be wrong. It can't be right. I can't possibly have fallen in love with the Italian mafia Don at first sight. If that's true, then I'm screwed.

"However I want? No limits?" he repeats, raising an eyebrow at me. I nod. The not-so-subtle smirk tugging at his lips tells me he's pleased by my words. Then he leans down, the sudden closeness causing me to purse my lips and suck in a breath. "How did you know I love doing whatever I want to punish people without having to stop?"

Without having to stop? I hope that extends to his vigour in bed, too.

The moment the thought crosses my mind, my eyes widen in shock. Really, what's wrong with me? Am I sick?

"David," he calls out as he looks over my head. I turn my head, watching as the little man scrambles to his feet. "Why don't you go with my boys and let them escort you to my estate? We can speak after the party's over."

His eyes widen in fear, but before he can say a word of protest, two big burly men appear out of nowhere and grab onto his arms. Alessandro nods their way, and then they proceed to drag a screaming and kicking David out of the room.

"Oh, he's so loud," Alessandro complains, running his fingers through his tousled hair. It looks like he didn't put any effort into taming those wild tresses, even for tonight.

I have no idea what to do or say. What can I possibly do or say in this situation, especially when I'm unsure of how he'll react.

He could be cool about this and just move on, or he could blow up on me and have two of his burly guards *escort* me to his estate as well, just like they did to David just now. The mere thought of what they — of what *he* — might do to him tonight makes me shudder. Something tells me it'll entail a lot of torturing, perhaps knives, guns, and blood. Lots and lots of blood.

"Adia Hamilton, am I correct?" he finally says, breaking through my train of thought. I almost shake my head at the name he addresses me by, but luckily, I manage to stop myself just in time, although I doubt I can muster something coherent out right now. So, instead, I just nod. "I must thank you for sending me a picture of your dress beforehand. Otherwise, I would have hesitated in thinking that you came here with someone else. But I must say, you look a lot different than I pictured you to look."

I freeze.

"Prettier, too," he murmurs. My head snaps up to his, my eyes widening. Did he just call me pretty? I think he did. Either that or this love-at-first-sight thing must be getting the better of me.

"I . . ." I trail off, pondering over my words. "I have to use the bathroom."

And without another word, I gather the poofy sides of my dress in between my fingers and scurry away from him, heading to an unknown bathroom. Luckily, after ending up in an empty hall on the side of the ballroom, I can vaguely see the sign of the bathroom hanging from the wall. I rush to the sign, push open the door, and slump against the sink by the mirror.

I bring my gaze up to the mirror, my eyes catching sight of myself in it. Pretty, he said. Would he still think I'm pretty after I take all this make-up off and discard this expensive dress for a pair of sweats? I'm not sure, but something in my gut tells me no.

Wait. Why am I even thinking about this? Why do I even care whether the Italian mafia Don finds me pretty or not?

I came here to ruin any chance there is of Alessandro picking me, well, Adia, to be his bride. That's the plan. That was the plan, but suddenly, after setting my eyes on him and listening to his sultry voice call me that name, the line between love and fear blurred ever so slightly.

No. I came here with a plan, a goal, an objective. If I fail in ruining things with Alessandro, Adia will kill me, although not before I kill myself for being so foolish. There's no chance for what I'm thinking of to happen. Yes, he called me pretty, but that's merely on a surface level. It doesn't mean he's interested in me, and what I felt when I looked at him can't be anything more than pure infatuation, either.

It was just a moment of weakness for me. That's all. I'm Havyn Miller, after all. I don't get swayed by good looks.

Suddenly, the bathroom door opens and two girls come walking in, not even sparing me a single glance. They immediately come to stand next to me by the mirror and pull items of make-up out of their purses.

"Did you see him?" the one with golden brown hair and brown eyes speaks. I resist the urge to roll my eyes at them. I honestly don't like girls who only know to gossip about other girls and have only one thing on their minds — boys. I'm about to walk away, but then I hear them mention *his* name.

"Alessandro Romano," the one with dirty blonde locks of hair and crystal blue eyes says. "He got even sexier since the last time I saw him. I didn't think it was possible to get sexier than that, but he proved me wrong."

I purse my lips, resisting the urge to listen to the nagging voice in my head screaming at me to ignore them and just leave the bathroom. I'm not sure what it is, but the mere mention of him has me frozen in my spot with ears willing to listen to just about anything.

"Did you see Aliya?" the brown-haired girl asks.

Aliya?

The blonde-haired girl rolls her eyes. "She has some nerve

to show up here. Why did they even let her in here in the first place?" she practically growls, her eyes alight with anger.

"Alessandro must've pitied her and let her in," the brunette exclaims, her lips forming a pout. "It's such a shame, though. She's not even worth his time, yet he's too sweet to just leave her hanging like she deserves."

"I hate that wench for having a piece of that meat before I did. I mean, how dare she when he's rightfully mine?" the blonde-haired girl growls, glaring into the mirror. Piece of meat? Is Alessandro the piece of meat? Well, I guess it's not that farfetched to call him that.

"Excuse me," I blurt out, my eyes widening once I realise what I've done. Both their eyes snap to mine. What in the world is wrong with me? "Uh . . . I couldn't help but overhear what you guys were talking about."

I bite my lower lip in nervousness, unsure of how these two girls will react to me suddenly butting into their conversation.

"Who are you?" the brunette asks, her voice sickly sweet.

"Ha-Adia Hamilton," I end with an awkward cough. I really need to stop doing that. Their eyes simultaneously widen.

"Adia Hamilton? As in Robert Hamilton's daughter?" the brunette exclaims.

I nod, suddenly feeling uncomfortable under their scrutinising eyes that now scan me from head to toe, as if they're judging whether I fit the profile Adia's father must have set up for her. Alessandro had a different picture, too, no doubt there, since I look nothing like the real Adia Hamilton. And there's the fact that he said it in so many words. He finds me pretty, though.

I have to stop myself when I feel my lips tugging upwards into a smile. Really, what's wrong with me? Why? Why of all people, does getting called pretty by him make me feel so warm inside? It's not the first time I've been called pretty. Adia calls me pretty all the time. So why is this time different?

Why is *he* different?

"But if you really are his daughter, what are you doing here?" the blonde-haired girl questions, narrowing her eyes at me. "I mean, since when does Robert Hamilton have business with the mafia?"

I don't answer immediately. What do I say? What can I say that won't make them suspicious of me?

"Since they formed a merger," I blurt out, internally cursing myself afterwards. "My dad is going to launder all the mafia's money through his business to clean it."

Please let this not come back to bite me in the future. I just spoke without thinking.

"Really?" the brunette pipes out, her brown eyes big. I nod, and she smiles. "Well then. What part of our conversation were you interested in?"

"Something about Aliya and Alessandro," I mutter, biting my lower lip.

The two girls exchange glances before finally bringing their attention back to me.

"They're ex-lovers," the brunette reveals, cringing underneath the blonde girl's harsh glare.

"They're not ex-lovers," she pipes out. "They were never lovers. They just had a brief . . . tryst."

"Okay. So why did they end their . . . tryst?" I carefully ask, treading over my words.

"Because she wasn't worthy of him, of course," the blonde boldly says with a scoff. "I don't know what he even saw in her in the first place."

"She was a virgin," the brunette pipes out, staring pointedly at her friend. "You know how much he loves virgins."

I shudder. That's disgusting, to say the least. Suddenly, I hate the fact that I'm still a virgin. Would he take advantage of me if he knew?

"Why?" I dare ask, although I know I probably won't like

the answer.

"It's the thrill of it," the blonde girl says, folding her arms across her chest. "It's a challenge, defiling a virgin girl and stripping her of all her innocence."

My face scrunches up in disgust. That doesn't sound nice at all.

"Oh, we didn't even introduce ourselves. Silly us. I'm Aubrey," the brunette introduces before pointing at her blonde friend. "And this is Savannah."

I nod, plastering a smile onto my face.

"So what are you guys doing at this party?" I decide to ask. I've asked enough about Alessandro and this Aliya girl now.

"Oh, actually . . . we're gate-crashing," Aubrey admits, taking a step closer to me. "Savannah's father got us into the party with his connections despite not being invited."

Of course their families are influential, as well. No one at this party is like me. Why did I ever think any differently?

"Why are you gate-crashing, though?" I can't help but ask, my eyebrows furrowing in confusion. Aubrey and Savannah share one hesitant glance before Savannah nods, and they both turn back to me.

"Because Savannah's in the running to be Alessandro's bride."

Chapter Seven: Havyn

Savannah's what?

"I'm sorry, what?" I blurt out, blinking at the two of them. Bride?

"Okay. Not many people know of this so don't go around telling people," Aubrey says, her voice turning hush. "Alessandro's reaching a . . . good age, and his father wants him to get married and have children, the heirs to the mafia throne if you want to call it that. But Alessandro isn't really interested in getting married, so his father arranged for him to meet multiple women on different occasions, and he's meant to choose the one he likes the most to wed. Savannah's one of those women."

I can't even blink.

"Tonight's technically not my night to spend with Alessandro, but I couldn't stop myself," Savannah admits.

"Savannah, you see, has had the biggest crush on Alessandro since she first saw the picture of him, and it's been her goal to marry him ever since then," Aubrey informs.

This is a lot to let sink in. Savannah, a potentially snobby rich girl, is gate-crashing my supposed date with Alessandro because she's secretly in love with him. How would she feel if she knew that I'm the one on a date with him tonight? Can I even call tonight a date? I've barely spoken one single sentence to him. But who knows? Maybe I'm lucky, and Alessandro already decided that he doesn't want me to be his bride. Then, at least Savannah is off my case.

"I'm planning to woo him with my beauty tonight, and

when we meet for our date, he'll think of it as fate." Savannah beams, her cheeks flushing with colour.

That sounds like a good idea on her part, especially since she's so pretty. I'm pretty, too, though, not that it matters. In the end, she comes from a wealthy family, and I don't, so it's obvious who he'll pick.

"So what are you hoping to get out of tonight?" Aubrey suddenly asks, my eyes snapping to hers. "Are you planning to bind business ties with the mafia instead of your father, or what? I mean, it's obvious why he sent you. With your beauty, you can make any man fall to his knees."

Savannah pouts at Aubrey's words. Why does this feel like yet another *Snow White* moment in my life? She's not going to drag a magic mirror out of her pocket, is she? No, of course not, because that would be ridiculous, almost as ridiculous as the fact that I'm here right now.

"Not Alessandro, though," Savannah pipes out, crossing her arms with a satisfied smirk on her face. I have to bite my tongue to stop myself from telling her how he called me pretty. That's adding unnecessary flames to this fire.

"Sure, sure," Aubrey half-heartedly mutters, patting her friend on the back. Savannah brushes her off, scrunching her face up at her.

"Have you guys eaten yet?" I question, trying to cut through the sudden tension in the room.

"No. We're watching our figures," Savannah says with a pout.

"She means she is. I'm not looking to impress any guys tonight," Aubrey says, taking a step closer to me. "So, what do you want to eat?"

She seems eager, but I'm not sure if she'll want to eat what I want to eat. Rich people don't eat what I eat. If I wasn't Adia's best friend, she wouldn't have even known what a cheeseburger was.

"What do you have in mind?" I ask instead. She hums, tapping her chin.

"Well, we could sneak out and get some greasy food with a lot of calories," she suggests, a mischievous glint in her eyes.

"You know a few places?" I ask, my eyes lighting up. I know all the good places that sell good fast-food, but I don't want to come off as a know-it-all. Not when I'm trying not to blow my cover. Aubrey opens her mouth to answer, but Savannah's quick to cut in.

"Guys," she cuts in. "Have you forgotten that I have to stay here all night? You can't just leave me alone here!"

"Doesn't us leaving you here alone give you a better chance with Alessandro?" Aubrey notes. "There wouldn't be any distractions."

Also, I could ditch the date, and that'll definitely set Alessandro off about me, and that means that there's no chance he'll choose me to be his bride. *Score.*

"Still," she insists. "You can leave after I meet him."

How long will that take? I need to leave immediately if I don't want them to find out that I'm Alessandro's date tonight.

"Fine," Aubrey relents with a sigh. "We'll have to go later, Adia."

I nod, trying not to show my distaste for this sudden situation on my face. Maybe I can just hide out in the bathroom while they find a way for Savannah and Alessandro to naturally meet. But then Aubrey grabs my hand, flashing me a smile. "Let's go."

I don't have a chance to protest before she pulls me out of the bathroom with them. However, the moment we step out of the bathroom, I hear an unfamiliar voice yell out a familiar name.

"Alessandro!"

All three of our heads snap up to the source of the voice.

My eyes widen when they land on Alessandro standing at the end of this very hall with a girl, a pretty girl, but she's crying with tears rolling down her face.

"Please, just listen to me," she begs, staring up at him with teary eyes.

"What now, Aliya?" he mutters with a light sigh. Aliya? Aliya . . . the girl Savannah and Aubrey were talking about. Alessandro's ex-lover. Something about that puts a bitter taste in my mouth.

"Why are you doing this? Why are you marrying someone else?" she chokes out.

"I told you. I have to get married to a suitable woman who comes from a suitable family to have heirs with," he simply says, staring at her as though he doesn't understand why she doesn't understand.

"But . . . but we love each other," she says, her eyebrows furrowing. *Love.* They love each other. I find myself biting my lip to the point that I can taste blood in my mouth. This feeling, is it jealousy? How can I possibly be jealous when what I'm feeling is merely an infatuation?

"I told you from the start, Aliya. We would see one another, but when the time came for me to take a wife, we would go our separate ways and never cross paths again," he reminds her. She chokes up in a sob.

"I only agreed because I thought that you would change your mind once you loved me," she admits.

"Nothing can change my mind, ever, especially not something as mundane and pitiful as love," he says, enunciating every single word.

"But I love you, Alessandro," she insists on saying, taking a step forward and taking his tattooed hand into hers. "We can make it work."

"No, we can't," he disagrees, pulling his hand out of hers.

"Yes, we can," she insists. "We can run away together. Go

live somewhere far away where no one will find us."

He scoffs. "You really think I'll leave everything to run away with you? Leave my empire that I worked so hard to build? You must be out of your mind."

At this point, he's glaring at her.

"But ... but we spent three years together," she argues, her bottom lip trembling. "How can you just give three years of your life up that easily?"

Three years? That means they started seeing one another when I was merely 15 years old. Somehow, my being here on this date with him seems a lot more illegal than I initially thought. How old is he even?

"Three years is nothing in this line of work. I've moved on," he says, causing her to flinch. He's doing this on purpose, to hurt her, I realise. Even though he made this clear from the beginning, there is no reason for him to hurt her so blatantly right now.

"Serves her right," Savannah pipes out, a little too loudly, and within a quick moment, both Alessandro and Aliya's heads snap to ours. The moment Alessandro's eyes meet mine, mine widen, and I immediately spin around, but not quick enough as I immediately hear him call out to me.

"Amore mio?"

That stupid nickname. He doesn't even know me, so why is he calling me that? Because I'm most definitely not his *love*. At least not in any other place than my mind, which dares to blatantly betray me in this moment.

Aubrey and Savannah's attention snap to mine, Aubrey's with shock and Savannah's with eyes that ask me *how the hell does he know you?* I shake my head at them, pleading at them, but then within a few moments, I feel a strong presence be-hind me. I feel *him* behind me.

"Why are you looking away from me?" he demands.

I purse my lips, slowly twisting around to face him.

"Hello," I awkwardly greet. His eyebrows furrow at my sudden greeting, but I just look straight at his chest, not risking meeting his eyes again. That's way too dangerous for me and for my heart right now.

"Is that her?" Aliya suddenly demands, coming to stand next to him. She's so tall standing next to him, much taller than me. "Is she who you moved on from me with?"

Alessandro releases a frustrated breath, not even looking at her as he utters, "It doesn't matter whether I'm seeing her or not because that is none of your business as we're done with each other. Understand?"

She whimpers at the tone of his voice.

Suddenly, the need to leave becomes apparent in the way sweat starts to accumulate in the palms of my hands, so I awkwardly clear my throat, holding my hand up in the air and saying, "Well, goodbye."

I turn around and start to walk away, but I'm not hardly quick enough, because a hand shoots out almost immediately and comes to grab my hip, and then I'm pulled flush against Alessandro's hard chest. My body stills against his.

"And where do you think you are going, *amore mio*?" he questions in a low voice. My eyes meet Savannah's and Aubrey's, and Aubrey portrays more confusion than anything else. I nearly flinch at Savannah's glare, which burns right through my skull and then through Alessandro's hand, which grips my hip in a way that tells me he's not planning on letting go anytime soon. If I were him, I wouldn't either, because the moment he lets go, I'm making a run for it. "If I'm not mistaken, we're on a date, and the moment I spoke to you for the first time, you made an excuse to use the bathroom. Then I waited, and now that you're out, you want to leave again?"

He waited for me? Is that why he's here in the first place? I thought it was to speak with Aliya in private. Speaking of Aliya, she hasn't said a word since he told her off. However, even though her eyes are filled with more fear now than sadness, they remain fixed on Alessandro's hold on me, just like Savannah's.

"I . . . uh . . ." I have no excuse.

"Thought so," he says, spinning me around in his arms so that I face him now. "Now, what do you want to do? Do you want to stand here in awkward silence, or do you want to come with me?"

He holds out his inked hand to me, and as he does, I can't help but analyse the tattoos that litter his skin. There's so many strokes and patterns and swirls on his skin that I can't even begin to comprehend what it all means, yet somehow, they all fit perfectly together, as if on purpose. I have no doubt they were.

I'm considering my options. I can stand here and possibly get my hair ripped out by both Savannah and Aliya while Aubrey watches me with pity, or I can go with Alessandro. The latter never seemed more appealing to me. And so, without wasting a moment longer, I place my hand on his, his fingers immediately coming to lace themselves in between my own, the feeling of his smooth yet rough, calloused skin causing me to shiver. Since when did I find even this tiny little detail attractive?

I'm not one of those girls who have their perfect match planned out up until the size of their pinkie toe, yet here I am, finding rough hands attractive. Perhaps it's what it indicates that makes it attractive. Hard labour. Although, I can't think of any other labour than killing others, but I guess that on its own has its . . . problems, I guess?

Without wasting another second, Alessandro pulls me to his side and pushes past Aliya before leading us away. I'm not sure where we're going, but I remain silent, wordlessly following him wherever he wants to take me. This is dangerous for me, especially since the option that he's leading me to my doom still sounds quite plausible. I can only hope that if he intends to murder me tonight, he'll make it quick so that I won't feel too much pain.

"Are you taking me someplace where you can kill me without alarming the guests?" I blurt out without thinking. Trust me to have no filter.

"I wasn't thinking about killing you until you just said that," he says.

My eyes widen. Oh no. What did I just do? He chuckles when he sees my reaction, shaking his head.

"Well, if you're going to do it, can you make it quick?" I can't help but request, adding fuel to the fire I somehow managed to start. "Just one shot to the head is all I ask."

"I'm not killing you," he says, a certain lightness in his voice, as if he's amused by me.

"Well, I'm glad you find my fear amusing," I retort, internally cursing myself afterwards. Adia warned me not to act this way with Alessandro. She also told me not to mention killing in front of him, yet here we are. Why can't I just learn to keep my mouth shut?

"I'm glad you're not boring." he retorts back.

"Boring? Why on earth would you think I would be boring?" I ask incredulously.

"It might just sound like I'm stereotyping, but I'm really not. Rich girls born with silver spoons are boring," he says, his tone telling me that he truly believes this. "If anything, the most interesting topic you'll get out of them is what sex positions they like."

I choke. He abruptly stops, turning to me with furrowed eyebrows.

"Why would you say that?" I exclaim. My question appears to confuse him even further.

"Say what?"

"You know . . ." I trail off, making a weird gesture with my hand that even I don't know the mean of. "The sex thing." I cringe at the sound of my own voice. I sound so childlike, and it's definitely not something Adia would say, so why did I say it? Why couldn't I just ignore what he said and move on? No, of course I couldn't. I never can when it comes to him, it seems.

"The . . . sex thing?" he repeats, amusement laced in his voice. I internally sigh. "What are you, five?"

No, I'm seventeen, almost eighteen in a few weeks, but still seventeen nonetheless, I guess.

I purse my lips, avoiding his eyes as I refuse to say anything further. What Savannah and Aubrey said about how much he likes defiling virgins isn't forgotten by me, and I can't trust him not to try anything if he knows about my still untorn hymen.

Wait, speaking of age . . .

"How old are you?" I question. It's honestly something that's been weighing on my mind. He doesn't answer for a few long moments, simply staring at me, and the intensity of his gaze causes me to lower mine.

"Twenty-eight."

Well, shit.

CHAPTER EIGHT: HAVYN

This is highly illegal.

Not only is he ten years older than me, but I'm also not even eighteen yet. I'm not legal yet! Well, it was nice speaking to him.

"You're twenty-three, right?" he questions, a certain undertone of suspicion in his voice, almost like he's daring me to say otherwise. Yes, twenty-three, Adia's age. One might think that the fact that Adia's five years older than me is strange, since we're best friends. There's no true explanation as to how our friendship came about. It just . . . happened.

"Yes." I nod, swallowing uncomfortably. He hums, tapping his chin as he appears to think. Well, the big age gap just made this entire situation with him very awkward on my part. I thought it would be reassuring to know that if he tries anything with me, he'll be arrested for touching a minor. However, I know that that won't happen, not when he basically owns the police.

"Let's go, Adia," he says, before continuing to pull me away with him. This action reminds me that not once did he let go of my hand when we spoke. He held on tightly. I'm not sure where we're going until we walk through a pair of tall gates that I quickly realise is the back exit when we step onto an empty alleyway. A car waits at the end of the alleyway. Well, this isn't suspicious at all.

Warning bells start ringing in my head, and I pull back against Alessandro's grip, causing him to stop. "Where are we going? Where are you taking me?"

38

"Wherever you want to go," he murmurs, his voice like a whisper in the cold night air.

"Are you joking?" I can't help but snap. If he's playing with me, then it's not funny. He shakes his head.

"Why would I joke?" he questions, tilting his head to the side slightly. Why wouldn't he? And then he takes a step forward, his voice lowering as he says, "Tell me, *amore mio*. Where do you wish to go? I'll take you."

"Is this because of our date, because that was supposed to be at the party, which means that the moment we stepped through those gates, the date came to its end?" I note, staring pointedly at him.

"No. The date ends when I say so," he simply says. "So tell me where you want to go."

He's not going to let up, I quickly realise, and besides, what's the point in playing this cat and mouse game with him? I'm clearly at a disadvantage here.

"Fine," I relent. "I'll tell the driver the address."

He nods, a certain expression painting his features. He's pleased. Of course he is. He won.

He pulls me to the sleek black car, opening and holding the door for me to get in. Such chivalry. I climb into the car, my bottom sinking into the surprisingly warm leather seat. Of course he has seat warmers. Alessandro follows after me, closing the door behind him. I lean forward slightly to tell the driver where I want to go, and even though he looks slightly surprised at the location I've just told him, he nods nonetheless and starts up the engine before taking onto the road.

"Where's this place?" Alessandro asks, leaning back against the seat.

I smile. "You'll see."

I'm quite pleased with what I've done, and I don't feel an ounce of guilt. He said he would take me wherever I wanted to go, so I'm not doing anything wrong.

The ride is quick, and before I know it, we're pulling up in front of one of my favourite fast-food restaurants in the city. I don't have to look at Alessandro to know how confused he must be right now, and I don't wait for him, climbing out of the car. He follows after a few long moments of what I assume was contemplation, his eyes scanning over the entrance of the restaurant.

"Where exactly have you brought us?" he asks as I round the car and come to stand next to him.

"One of my favourite places," I say, breathing in the cold air.

"A fast-food restaurant? I hardly think so," he mutters, unimpressed.

"Hey. You said wherever I wanted to go, and I want to be here," I say, tugging at his jacket sleeve as I lead him into the restaurant.

"How do you even know about this place?" he questions as I pull him to the front counter.

"A friend," I simply say, smiling at the woman behind the counter.

"What do you want?" she asks.

"Nothing," he mutters, sending an unimpressed glance my way. I roll my eyes at him.

"I'd like two classic burgers with extra cheese, please," I say, and she nods, typing my order onto the machine. When the time comes to pay, I turn to Alessandro expectantly. "Your card, sir."

"Why the hell should I pay? I don't even want to be here," he grumbles.

"Well, this is still a date, so you're paying. It's only right," I say, staring pointedly at him. He glares at me before digging into his suit jacket pocket and pulling out a black leather wallet. He flips it open and grabs one of the many black cards before handing it to me. I smile at the woman, insert the card into the card machine, and then gesture for him to type in his card pin.

He doesn't type it in. Instead, he leans down to me and whispers into my ear, "When's your birthday?"

"My birthday?" I repeat, and he nods. "October fifteen."

He nods before taking out his phone and clicking onto the screen a few times. I can't see what he's doing, though since he's too tall. Then he stops, placing his phone back into his pants pocket, and starts typing on the machine. I can't help but peek over, reading the numbers out in my mind. 1-0-1-5. 1015. 1015 . . . 1015?

My . . . that's my birthday.

My head snaps up to his, my eyebrows furrowing in confusion, and my eyes wide. He turns to me, shrugging as he says, "I never had a meaningful pin before now, and now I do."

What does that even mean? My birthday's meaningful to him?

"Why?" I can't help but ask, my voice soft and small. His mouth quirks.

"Because I like you."

My breath hitches in my throat. He . . . likes me? He likes *me*? Me, of all people?

"Why?" I can't help but ask again.

"Because you're pretty," he half-heartedly says, as if that's one of the many reasons he likes me. But really, why?

"Your food will be with you shortly," the woman behind the counter suddenly says, startling me out of my thoughts. Alessandro nods, grabbing my hand once more and pulling me to a secluded booth in the corner of the restaurant. He sits down, and I slip into the seat opposite his.

He likes me. Alessandro likes me. Oh, why is that all I can think about? I must be losing my mind. Alessandro slips his card back into his wallet, and just before he closes the wallet,

I notice something sticking out on the side of it. A photo. A photo of someone I know all too well now.

Aliya.

My mood deflates, and I can't help but frown. Yes, he rejected her, but him having a photo of her in his wallet says a lot. He's clearly not over her yet, so why in the world is he telling me he likes me? Is he playing with me?

"Bad jerk," I angrily mutter, kicking the leg of the table. He's such a jerk. Oh no, can he tell that I might be interested in him? For now, I'm labeling it as infatuation, but the depression at seeing a photo in his wallet of another woman he dated for three years tells me otherwise.

"What's wrong?" he questions, his eyebrows furrowing in confusion. I scoff. Does he really not know? How can he not know?

"Nothing," I mutter, glaring up at him.

"*Amore mio,*" he calls out.

I ignore him.

"*Amore mio,*" he calls out again.

I ignore him.

"Havyn!"

My head snaps up, my eyes widening.

"What . . . what did you just call me?" I slowly ask, my voice filled with disbelief.

"I called you *amore mio,* but since you didn't respond, I called you by your name. Adia," he answers, glaring down at me. Adia. He called me Adia, so why did I hear him call me by *my* name?

"Here's your food." The same woman suddenly appears at our booth, placing our burgers and fries in front of us. She flashes us both a smile. "Enjoy."

She walks away, and I shake my head. I need to gather myself. I'm starting to slip. So I plaster a fake smile onto my face, saying, "Try it. I think you'll really like it."

He doesn't respond, staring at me as though he can tell that my smile is fake, but he peels off the packaging of the burger and takes a bite of it nonetheless. The frown on his face remains. However, after a few chews, it slowly disappears, being replaced with pure surprise.

His eyes lift to mine for a brief moment before he takes another bite. I can't help but smile at his reaction. My smile is real this time. Why is he so darn sexy yet cute at the same time? And why in the world do I notice all these small things about him? Oh my . . .

Am I really interested in him?

CHAPTER NINE: HAVYN

I like him.

For some inexplicable and unknown reason, I like Alessandro Romano, the Italian mafia Don. I must have lost my mind.

This is bad. Having feelings for someone like him is like signing your own death warrant. This isn't good. Not at all.

"This is good," Alessandro suddenly says, taking his last bite of his burger. I smile up at him. He must have really liked it, considering the fact that he basically scarfed the entire thing up in like one minute. "Can I have yours?"

Surprise flashes through me. He wants mine, too?

"Sure. Have at it," I say, sliding my burger over to him. He doesn't say anything or give any reaction, just opening the packaging and biting into the bun. He finishes this one in no time, too, nodding in satisfaction afterwards.

I like him. *I'm screwed.*

"I have to admit, I'd come here again," he says, wiping his mouth with a napkin. I smile, oddly satisfied by this.

"I'm glad," I say, leaning back in my seat. "I intend to please."

"You're cute," he suddenly murmurs, my gaze snapping to his in surprise.

"W-what?" I splutter out. What about what I just said was cute?

Alessandro chuckles, his eyes darkening. "I believe beautiful is the more appropriate term."

I'm speechless. Nothing comes out of my mouth, and I'm left staring at him like a bewildered fish out of water. He called me beautiful. Nothing else matters.

"Cat got your tongue, my love?" he teases, tilting his head to the side slightly. I shake my head, blinking out of whatever trance I was in.

"You wish," is all I can snap back. He got me. Dammit.

He chuckles, his green eyes sparkling underneath the restaurant lights as he shakes his head from side to side. The action leaves me frozen in amazement, and I can't help but ogle him and take in every feature. The way his pink lips part as he laughs, the way his silky jet-black strands shake and fall effortlessly onto his head and forehead. Everything . . . everything about him is beautiful, breathtakingly beautiful.

I'm stuck in such a deep trance that I fail to notice when he stops laughing, and it's only when his previously light-filled green eyes darken that I snap out of it. I want to break our stare, but I can't seem to look away. The way he stares at me, it's almost as if he's devouring me with his eyes. It makes me shiver with desire. It's a never felt sensation travelling down south.

I should feel embarrassed. I really should, but how can I when he stares down at me with such a hunger aflame in his eyes? I can only hope I don't mimic his look. Although I'm almost ninety per cent sure I am.

"Come back to my place with me," he murmurs, his voice thick with desire, and it's all it takes to snap me back to reality. Suddenly, it's like a bucket of ice-cold water has been dumped over me. What in the world was I just doing?

I stand abruptly from my seat. "I-I have to go."

I grab my purse with hasty fingers and turn out of the booth. However, I barely move more than a single inch before I feel a warm hand wrap around my wrist, pulling me to a stop. I don't dare turn to him, keeping my back to him. I can't look at him. I'll falter if I do.

"What's the matter now, *amore mio?*"

The lack of anger in his voice surprises me. He does, however, sound quite frustrated, like he can't possibly understand me. How can he, when even I confuse myself with the mixed signals I find myself casting his way?

"Let me go." It takes everything in me to utter these words and not sound heartbroken as I do. Why am I feeling like this when I just met the man tonight? Is this really love at first sight? If so, people lie about it in novels. In novels, they describe it as something positive and heart-warming, but I've been in pain ever since my first encounter with this man.

Alessandro's hold on my wrist loosens, and I take that opportunity to pull away from him completely and dart out of the restaurant. A part of me wants to stop and turn back and run into his arms. A part of me wants to be selfish, but I can't, not when Adia's entire future rides on tonight.

A traitorous tear rolls down my cheek, and I'm quick to wipe it away. I'm so stupid. How could I let myself be swayed by something as simple as feelings by a man like him? I'm just about to pass the car we came here in when suddenly an arm wraps itself around my waist, and I'm spun around, my body crashing into a hard chest.

I don't even bother fighting against his hold, my body voluntarily surrendering to his touch. Adia will never forgive me for this. My body trembles against his, tear after tear rolling down my cheeks.

"Talk to me, *amore mio*," Alessandro murmurs into my hair, his fingers brushing my face. "Tell me what's wrong."

A light bulb goes off in my head. This is it. I can end it all now. And so I do, forcing the lying words out of my mouth.

"I don't want to get married to you."

Chapter Ten: Havyn

"I'm proud of you."

Ever since I walked through the gates of the estate Adia lives in, Adia hasn't stopped thanking and praising me. I haven't uttered a single word since I got here, yet somehow, she knows that I messed up the date, and she's happy. She's happy. I helped my best friend.

So why do I feel so empty inside?

I hate this feeling. This emptiness, this loneliness. Having spent most of my life alone, I'm used to it now. Yet why? Why do I feel so lonely after saying goodbye to Alessandro? No, I know why. It's the way he looked at me after I uttered those tearful words.

"I don't want to get married to you."

He tensed against me, his strokes on my head coming to a halt. He wasn't expecting to hear my rejection. His hands gripped my arms, pushing me back a little bit so that he could look at me.

"Why?" he uttered. "Why do you say that?"

"Because it's true," I said, unable to look him in the eyes.

"Is it because you fear me? Because of who I am and what I do for a living?" he questioned.

"No," I bit out, my tear-filled eyes raising to meet his. "I just don't like you."

I lied. I lied, and even though I begged him to protest against my words with my eyes, he believed me, and he relented, his hands leaving me and falling down to his sides.

"Fine," he finally said after a few moments of long silence. "I

won't choose you."

No, choose me, my heart yelled out. But the words failed me.

"But," he added, hesitating for a few moments. "Don't ever think that this is the end."

My eyebrows furrowed in confusion. What was he talking about? How could that not be the end, when we would certainly never cross paths after that night?

Then suddenly, his hands grasped my face, pulling me up slightly so that I was forced to stand on my tiptoes. "I never let go of something I want."

His words were full of promise. Something he wanted, could that possibly be me?

"So tonight, I'll let you go, but this is far from over," he said.

"Why?" I mumbled. "Why won't you let me go?"

This all felt oddly emotional, considering the fact that we had only met that very night. Why did it feel like I was saying goodbye to a long-lost lover of mine?

"Because I hardly like anyone," he admitted. "But you . . . even after just spending one night with you, I like you. You intrigue me to the point that I don't want to say goodbye to you. But because I like you, I will do as you request, just for tonight."

My heart felt constricted, both in a good and bad way. He was interested in me as I was him, but then again, would he still feel that way after finding out who I really was? I vividly remember how he treated Aliya at the party. He treated her as though she was of no worth just because she wasn't a suitable partner for someone of his status, and they'd been together for three long years. All we had was one night, one really short night. I knew deep down that it wasn't enough, not nearly enough, to keep a man like him as mine.

"All right," I found myself saying, pushing down the negative thoughts brewing in my head and leaning upwards to wrap my arms around his neck. "Don't let me go. Not until I fall for you."

His eyes flashed with something I'd never seen before. I could barely believe what it was. Desire, desire for me.

"Okay," he said, his lips turning upwards ever so slightly. "I promise."

Then his hands were on my lower back, pulling me further up against him. My breath hitched. He was close, too close for me to be able to think properly.

"I want to kiss you," he suddenly admitted, my heart stopping in my chest. "But I won't, not until you want me to."

I want you to, my heart screamed, but the words refused to come out of my mouth. So I just nodded. And then he let me go.

So that's why I feel so lonely. Because I felt a moment in his arms, and now I don't want to be anywhere else. If I ever utter these words out loud, whoever I say them to will tell me the exact words that ring in my head. I'm screwed.

And now I feel guilty because not only did I lie to him, but I lied to her, too, my best friend. She thinks that it's all over now. That she won't have to worry about him being in her life any longer, but she's wrong, so very wrong, and it's all my fault. Since when was I so weak? Before setting my eyes on him, I was confident that I could tear him a new one, but now, I've been reduced to a soppy and feelings-ridden *girl*. What do I do with all these feelings now?

I've really messed things up for both Adia and myself by giving into my sinful desires for a man I barely know.

"So he won't bother us ever again?" Adia's voice pulls me out of my thoughts. I nod, swallowing the truth. He's not done, not with me. So for a little while, I might have to steal Adia's identity, just for a little while, until I can build up the guts to tell him the truth. Because the truth is, I want to see him again. And, as bad as it sounds, I want to be with him just once, just once before everything comes crashing down. Is it too much to ask for? Yes, but I can't even care anymore.

I want to be selfish, just this once. And I can only hope he won't hate me afterwards.

Chapter Eleven: Havyn

"Are you sure about this?"

I nod, clenching my hands into fists on my lap. Ms Blake sighs, shaking her head as she scribbles her signature across the form.

"I'm going to need your guardian's signature to process your dropout, though," she says. I curse under my breath. I was hoping and praying that she would let it slide, just this once.

"I don't have a guardian," I say, albeit hesitantly. I don't share with others, especially strangers. And even though she's been my homeroom teacher all year, I've never had a proper conversation with her. I'm not one to speak out in class or cause any trouble. I'm one to sit at the back of the class in the corner with my hoodie pulled over my head that no one bothers with. So this is my first real conversation with Ms Blake, even though I've been in her class for eight months already.

Ms Blake sighs, pulling out a yellow file from her desk drawer and flipping it open. She flips through the pages before finally stopping, her fingers pressing against the paper. There I am, at the top square block of the page, standing tall in my school uniform, a blank expression on my face with lips pursed into a thin line. I look so serious and unhappy, like I was forced to be there, which I was.

"It says here your mother has passed, but your father's still alive." She reads from the information page, sliding my dropout form across the desk back to me. I bite my lower lip. My father, yes, he's alive, but he hasn't been a part of my life for a while now. "Have him sign the form and bring it back to me."

"He can't," I force myself to say.

"And why not?" she asks, raising an eyebrow at me. Is she really going to make me say the words? No, there's no way I'm telling her the truth. I don't need her sympathy nor her second-hand pity. Worse, she'll cry and hug me, pretending that she understands.

"He's not around," is all I say. There's no reason for me to share my whole sob story with her.

"Where is he?" she shamelessly asks, batting her eyelashes innocently at me. I hold in my scoff. How dare she? She pretends to be so kind and understanding, yet just like everyone else, she's busy and wants to know everything about everyone.

"I don't want to tell you," I boldly say. She has no say over me and has no right to force me to tell her everything. She blinks in surprise, my words visibly taking her aback. I resist the urge to smile. She doesn't know me. To her, I'm that quiet student that never speaks, but I'm not just that. I just choose not to talk, and when I do, I don't hold anything back for anyone, especially not a busy middle-aged woman who thinks she's better than everyone else.

I've seen her. I've watched her. But she doesn't know that.

"In order for me to help you, I have to know," she says, leaning forward in her seat. When I don't respond, she adds, "If you continue to resist, you'll have to complete this year."

Resist? What is this? A fight?

I really don't want to finish this year, my final year. No, that's a lie. I do want to finish it. I want to have something behind my name, even if it's just grade 12. But life won't allow me to. Ever since being kicked out of my apartment, I've been spending all my savings, what little there is, on spending nights at a cheap motel near where I used to live while I search for an affordable place to move into, and that means one thing. I have to work extra shifts, meaning that I won't have time to attend school or do my homework. So the only option is dropping out.

I have no other choice.

"So?" Ms Blake cuts into my train of thought. "Are you going to get your father to sign the form, or are you going to complete the year? I advise that skipping classes and exams isn't ideal. It'll only cause you to fail, and that means that you will have to return next year. Do you want that?"

Dammit. She's got me.

"I'll finish the year," I finally say, defeat lacing my tone. I'll just have to manage, somehow.

She nods, a satisfied smile painting her features as she crumples up the dropout form in her hand and drops it into the bin next to her.

"I'll see you in class tomorrow," she says, and I nod, standing up from the seat. I nod my head goodbye before leaving her office and trudging down the empty hallway. Soon, after a few long moments of just walking, the bell rings and students come filtering out of the classrooms, none of them acknowledging me, just how I want it. But why do I feel so alone today?

I'm used to being alone, with no one by my side. But today? Today feels different for some reason.

I walk to my locker, inserting my pin on the lock before unlocking it and pulling the door open. Nothing. Nothing at all. My locker is completely empty. When was the last time I was here?

I'm about to close the locker when three girls appear at the locker two across from mine, and one pulls it open, the photo sticking to the inside of the door sending a shiver down my spine. It's no ordinary photo. No. It's a photo of a powerful person. *My* powerful person.

How did they even get that photo of him? Before that night, I'd never seen his face, and I'm certain if it wasn't for the situation and circumstances, I never would have.

God, I miss him. It's been two weeks since that night, our date, since he said he wouldn't let me go, and I haven't seen him since. He promised that he would come for me, but the chances of him finding *me* are slim. If he's even looking, the only person he'd find is Adia, the *real* Adia Hamilton. Not me, the fake, the clone, the substitute.

"You do realise that lusting after him when he doesn't even know you exist isn't going to do anything, right?" the blonde-haired girl says, staring pointedly at the redhead, the owner of the locker.

"She's right, you know. No matter how pretty you are or what family you come from, you're too young for him," the brunette adds.

I wince. That's right. The age gap. After constantly missing him for the past two weeks, that specific fact had slipped my mind. I'm not sure how, though, considering how much it bothered me when I first found out. Even if he manages to find *me*, there's no way we would work out because — other than the obvious reasons, such as who I really am and my current financial status — I'm too young for him. Way too young.

This is the first time I wish I'd been born sooner. Before, I liked being young. But now? It's more like a burden. But I have to be honest with myself. The biggest deal isn't even the age gap, no matter the fact that it's a complete decade. It's who I am, and who he is. He's the powerful Italian mafia Don, while me? I'm a teenage high school student with drowning debt to my name. If he didn't want Aliya despite having been in a relationship with her for three long years, why on earth would he want me?

I'm even less suitable for him than her.

Chapter Twelve: Alessandro

I miss her.

That girl . . . she's all I can think about. *Fuck.*

"Boss," a distant voice calls out, barely audible to my own ears. "He's here."

I sigh, nodding before signalling for him to leave. Moments later, another figure appears in the doorway. I watch him as he walks into my office and settles into the chair opposite me. He looks confident, but I can see through that façade. He's nervous. Of course he is. Why wouldn't he be?

Robert Hamilton. One of the most successful businessmen of this decade. He drowns in money, whether it be legal or illegal. But most of that money is mine. My money that he thinks I don't know he's been stealing from me. How could I not know, though? I'm not like other men who don't check their books to make sure everything adds up and entrusts their money to others. No, I don't trust anyone. Especially not with my money.

"May I ask what you called me here for, Mr Romano?" he speaks up, his eyes avoiding mine. He calls me Mr. Romano even though he's almost three decades my senior. Feels good.

I play with the silver banded ring on my index finger, twirling it around. I fight the urge to scoff at his question. He steals from me, and yet two weeks ago, he sends his daughter to me to wed. To my father, Adia Hamilton is the perfect candidate for me to wed in terms of where she comes from. She's also beautiful, meaning that we'd make striking children. But no, I don't agree. Adia Hamilton, who is she even? Maybe I would have cared if there wasn't a certain brunette clouding my brain.

That night two weeks ago, I was supposed to be going on a date with Adia Hamilton, and since my father was so dead set on me marrying her, I did research on her. And would you believe what I found? The first thing that popped up was pictures of her leaving clubs and entering hotel rooms with multiple women. So, obviously, that didn't make sense to me. Why would she agree to go on a date with me with the preposition of marriage dangling in the air if she didn't even find my gender attractive? Was she trying to play me? Trying to use me to please Daddy dearest?

There was no way I would allow myself to be used by a snotty rich girl. I use people, not the other way around. So of course, I pretended as though I didn't know anything. I wanted to meet her on that date and see just how far she was going to take her façade. And then I saw *her*. She was most definitely not Adia Hamilton, but Jesus, she was everything and even more. She was absolutely stunning, the most stunning woman I have ever seen in my life.

The moment I saw her walk into the room, wearing that dress Adia had sent me a picture of, my breath hitched. One could easily see that she didn't belong there, despite being the most beautiful of everyone present. At first, I was confused, obviously. Clearly, she wasn't the woman I was supposed to be meeting. No, she wasn't even a woman. She was a girl. Anyone with eyes could see how young she was, how inexperienced and naïve she was. But there she was, walking into a party filled with powerful criminals who could get rid of her with the mere snap of a finger.

I could practically feel the anxiety rolling off her in waves, and I had to fight the urge to smile at how she scrunched her face up at the fancy food in the buffet in the cutest way possible. No one at that party could see me smile.

For a few minutes, I was content with just watching her, but then *he* approached her. He touched her, that bastard. I have to be honest. For one single moment, I thought about not intervening, especially when I realised that she had quite the mouth on her, but then again, I knew David. He's a disgusting man, one who would go as far as stripping a girl naked in front of everyone and raping her. And there was no way I would let him do that to *her*, whoever she was.

So I stepped in. I'd never seen him look so terrified before in my life, especially when I touched her, electricity pulsing through my veins. When she turned to me, my heart stopped in my chest. How was it possible that she was even more breath-taking up close? I wanted to claim her in that very moment, in front of everyone. Never before had I felt a desire for someone so strong. And she looked so innocent. The way she stared up at me like she was afraid yet still thankful for me, and for a mere second, I don't think she realised, but desire flashed in her eyes. Desire for me.

I had to force myself not to kiss her that very moment. The nickname spilled from my lips. *Amore mio*. As a born Italian, I never called any of my previous lovers by pet names of my mother tongue. None of them were worth it. But with her, it didn't even require a single thought. It just came out of me, as though I'd called her that a thousand times before, so naturally. And then, when she told me to punish him in any way I wanted, something in me throbbed. I think in both my chest and pants.

I wanted to do whatever I wanted to her. Tie her up, choke her, touch her where I know she's never been touched before. I wanted to worship her body. I wanted to worship *her*. And that was bad, because I immediately knew that I didn't just want her to be a casual hook-up. I wanted more, and in my line of work, that's dangerous. Very dangerous.

"Mr. Romano?" Hamilton calls out, his voice uncertain.

He successfully pulls me out of my thoughts. I shake my head, snapping out of it.

"I went on a date with your daughter two weeks ago," I start by saying, and he nods, gulping. He wants me to choose his daughter to be my bride, so he's nervous I've called him here to reject her. "But unfortunately, I cannot marry her while her father's stealing from me."

He freezes, his eyes widening.

"What . . . what do you mean?" he stutters. "I haven't been stealing from you."

"Don't play with me, Robert," I snap. "I know you've been stealing my money for months now."

He visibly sweats, droplets of sweat trickling down his face.

"Now, I've let it go because of how long we've been working together, but if I'm to marry your daughter, it can no longer happen," I say.

"Wait. Are you saying you're interested in marrying my daughter?" he says, cutting in, his eyes widening.

No, I don't want to marry your daughter. I want her friend.

"I haven't made my decision yet," I say, leaning forward in my seat. "But if you want me to choose her, you can start making things right by paying me the two hundred thousand you owe me."

"If I pay you back, will you please marry her?" he asks, his eyes pleading. My eyebrow quirks.

"Why do you want me to marry your daughter so badly?" I question, my eyes narrowing on him.

"I just want her to have a good life without any struggles," he admits. "She has no worth as a businesswoman after I pass, so I don't want to have to worry about her even in the afterlife."

So she's useless, in plain words. All she has is her last

name. I know of someone who's worth so much more than her. *No, Alessandro. Don't go there.* No matter how hard it is, don't think about her.

"If you pay me back my money, I'll think about it." It's all I say. I'm not willing to make any promises. I'm not even sure I can marry her when all I can think about is her beautiful friend. Would she invite her to the wedding? No, let's not even think about that.

"Thank you," he says, breathing out, seemingly relieved that there's a chance. "I'll wire you the money immediately."

He stands up, dusting off his pants before walking to the door. "Also," he says, pausing at the door. "I apologise for stealing from you."

I'm itching to ask him why he did it in the first place, especially since I know he doesn't exactly need the money. His company is well off enough to support him for decades to come.

"One more thing," I say before he can make a move to leave. "Havyn Miller. Do you know her?"

"Havyn Miller?" he repeats. I nod. "She was Adia's friend, but she was too materialistic. Only wanted Adia for her money. So I gave her what she wanted. A hundred grand, and she was never to be seen again."

"Did she take it?" I slowly ask, hesitating slightly. He nods. My heart plummets to my stomach. Was I wrong about her? Did she take the money but still remain in Adia's life without Robert knowing? Would she only want me for my money, too? Someone like that would do anything for an extra buck. And I have more than enough for her to live a life of luxury. If she took the money, where did it go? But is her body enough for me to give her all that? What if I want more than that afterwards? What if I become greedy and want her heart, too?

Nothing scares me, but that thought alone scares me to my

core.

"Are you certain about this?" I can't help but ask, needing to be sure. I really don't want that to be her.

"I gave her the money in person, and she was more than willing to take it," he says, quirking an eyebrow at me. "I'm certain."

I look away from him, clenching my hands into fists on my desk. How could I have been so wrong about someone? Usually I can read people very well, and my assumptions of them are rarely wrong. Was I that blinded by her beauty to see through her lies and deceit?

I don't want to believe Robert's words. For some reason, I want to give her the benefit of the doubt, but I've known Robert for a long time now, and especially after me revealing to him that I know he's been stealing from me, he wouldn't lie to me. He has no reason to lie to me, not about her. Havyn Miller — the girl who hasn't escaped my mind once since I let her go that night.

I don't want to marry you, she said, but her eyes told me a different story. They were screaming at me. She wanted me just as much as I wanted her.

"Why are you asking about her, though?" he questions.

"We have some unfinished business," I simply say, not wanting to give too much away.

"No way. Did she get into trouble with the mafia?" he exclaims, his eyes widening. "I should've known. Someone as desperate as Havyn Miller would do anything for an extra buck."

My eyes darken. How can he say something like that about her? I'm so hypocritical, honestly. I thought the exact same thing about her minutes ago, but for some reason, hearing *him* speak about her like that makes my blood boil.

"Shut up," I snap, glaring him down from where I sit even though he stands. His eyes widen in fear. "Keep her name out of your mouth."

"Who is she to you?" he boldly asks, the fear still visible in his eyes.

Who is she to me? A one-night stand that I didn't even sleep with? More?

I immediately think of the nickname I called her. Is that who she is to me? My love? My love, Havyn Miller. Havyn Miller, my love.

"My love," I say before I even realise the weight of my words. My love. I really shouldn't have called her that in front of this bastard. How can I know he won't use this against me? I can't. And then my eyes darken. "So don't you dare touch her."

He gulps.

"She's poor, you know?" he interjects. "She's got nothing to her name. Your father will never approve of her."

He's right. If my father didn't even approve of Aliya, a woman from a fairly well-established family, he'll definitely reject Havyn without a second thought. And honestly, that bothers me more than I'd like to admit. Before this, I thought of myself as a man without feelings, and that's how I was able to reject Aliya even after spending three years together, but with her, this girl . . . something's different. I don't know why, but it is. I shouldn't care, but I do.

If my father doesn't approve, there's no way I can be with her, and that's why, despite how desperately I've wanted to, I haven't gone to her for the past two weeks, resorting to re-playing the one night we spent together in my head over and over again in order to not lose my mind missing her.

One night. That's all I have with her. So why in the world does she affect me this badly? I barely know the girl, and she lied to me about who she was. That's a red flag, yet I'm willing to overlook all that just to see her once more.

Should I just go to her and spend one long night with her?

Take her to my hotel and ravish her all night long? Would that get her out of my head?

Somehow, I don't think so.

Chapter Thirteen: Havyn

"Havyn, table four wants to order!"

I scramble to my feet, tossing my book carelessly onto the back counter and grabbing the notepad that I use to take orders before rushing over to table four. Luckily, the young couple sitting there are kind and quite easily accept my apology for making them wait. Why can't all customers be as understanding as them?

It's been about a week, five days to be exact, since I tried to drop out of school and failed in doing so. Things since then have been ... challenging, to say the least. Juggling both school and three jobs at the same time is difficult, especially on days like this where the café is packed with customers and I barely have a single minute to attempt doing my homework. It's maths today, meaning that I need to pay extra attention to what I'm doing, and between my manager and customers barking orders at me, I can't focus for a single moment.

Luckily, I've managed to secure myself a small apartment downtown, not too far from where I stayed before, so it's still within walking distance from the bus stop. It's tiny, the bedroom, kitchen, and living room all being in one space, but at least there, I'm the only one with a key to unlock the door. It's a relief that I no longer have to come home every night to weed and cigarette smells lingering in the air. My savings, however, have taken a huge dent in them, and if it wasn't for the daily tips I get at the café, which is barely anything in itself, I would be starving every night.

"Havyn!" a voice yelling snaps me out of my thoughts, and

I shake my head before turning to the source. My manager, Mrs. Dill, stares at me with her hands on her hips, unimpressed as she tips her head back, gesturing for me to come to her. I rush over to her, quickly tearing the page from my notebook and handing it to the chef. "Listen, I know that you have a lot on your plate right now, and I genuinely understand, but I can't have you slacking off."

"I apologise, Mrs Dill," I say, bowing my head down. Mrs Dill is a very understanding and patient woman, but when it comes to work, she's very strict, and for some reason, having her be angry at me makes me want to bow down in shame. She already has so much patience with me, allowing me to take little five-minute breaks to do my schoolwork, and I don't want her to feel that I'm taking advantage of her kindness.

"Havyn," she softly says, placing a hand on my shoulder. "If you feel that things are getting too much for you, just tell me. We can always find a replacement for you."

My eyes widen and my head snaps up, shaking profusely. "No. I'm quite fine. I'm coping. There's no need for you to find someone else. I'm very much capable of doing this job."

"I don't doubt your capability, Havyn," she assures. "I just know that you're in your final year of school and clearly, working this job is interfering with your studies. I'm just worried, is all."

"You don't have to worry, Mrs Dill. I'm okay. I'll get through this year just fine," I assure her. I pray she believes me because even I can hear the lie in my own ears. I can only hope she doesn't notice the tremble in my voice.

"All right," she says with a defeated breath. "Just let me know if you need help with anything."

I release a relieved breath when she walks away. *Help.* I need a lot of help, but I won't ask her for it, even if she's the closest thing I have to an actual present guardian. I don't like owing people because no matter how sincere they may seem, they always ask for something in return, whether it be immediately or in ten years' time. I can't add something like that to the debt I already have.

"Havyn, baby," a familiar voice calls out, and I whip around, a smile spreading across my face when my eyes meet hers. Instinctively, I feel the need to wrap myself in her arms and seek the motherly warmth she provides me with when I need it. And so I do, running into her awaiting arms like a lost child. I do feel lost, most of the time. "My, my. Did you miss me?"

Adia coos while she strokes my head in a soothing manner.

"It's been a tough week for you, huh?" she murmurs, and I sigh, closing my eyes. She knows. She always knows, even when we haven't seen one another in a week. It's not entirely my fault that we haven't seen one another, though. I've just been so swamped with work and school that I barely have time for myself, let alone her. I can't even remember the last time I cooked myself a proper meal for dinner. I've been surviving on cup noodles for the last three weeks, just barely. But Adia doesn't know how tough it's been for me lately. She still doesn't even know that I moved elsewhere. There was just never a right time to tell her, and I couldn't tell her I was kicked out. I'll just slide it into our conversation randomly at some point and then act like it's no big deal.

Finally pulling away after what feels like merely a few seconds, I ask, "What are you doing here?"

"Can't I come and check up on my best friend from time to time?" she questions, although amusement is visible in her eyes.

"Sorry. Of course, you can," I say, trailing my fingers across the wood of the front counter.

"What's up with you?" Adia immediately asks. She's clearly noticed that something's off with me.

"Nothing much. Just, school's becoming more hectic as we go further into the year." I shrug. I'm not exactly lying. I'm just not disclosing parts of the truth to her.

"I can imagine. I remember my senior year. People say it's fun. I didn't agree with any of them," she says with a fake shudder.

I smile.

"By the way, just to put you at ease, Alessandro hasn't bothered me or my father with a preposition to marry me, so I think it's safe to say he's off our backs."

My smile drops. Right. Alessandro. I'm not sure how, but any thought of him had completely slipped my mind due to how chaotic my week has been. It's a good thing, though, especially since it's been three weeks since the date, and he hasn't approached Adia thinking that she's me. That fact does hurt a little, though, because it means that I and that night were so insignificant for him that he forgot about the promise he made to me.

And even with all of that, I can't help but ask, "Do you know if he's chosen a wife yet?"

Adia shrugs, to my dismay. "I don't know, and I couldn't care less as long as it ain't me."

I also shouldn't care . . . but I do. God, I do. I do so much.

"Why do you ask, though?" Adia suddenly questions, raising an eyebrow at me. "If you're still worrying about him bothering me, you don't have to anymore. I mean, clearly, he's done with me."

Yes. Clearly, he's done . . . with me. That much is obvious now. I wouldn't be surprised if he's already married to some woman from a wealthy and prestigious family. Still, the thought hurts. Because deep down, I know that I want it to be me. I want to be the one he marries, the one he touches, the one he kisses, and the one he wakes up to every morning.

"Shit," is what I hear before I'm spun around, my back

facing Adia now.

"What? What's going on?" I question, trying to twist around in her hold, but she holds me in place with a firm grip.

"Don't turn around," she says, a certain seriousness overtaking her voice. "Shit, shit, shit. Why now, and why here of all places?"

"What's going on?" I exclaim, confused by her constant cursing and the worry that has now seeped into her voice.

Adia hesitates for a few moments before finally saying, "He's here."

Here? He? Who is here?

"Alessandro is here."

CHAPTER FOURTEEN: HAVYN

Alessandro is here.

My heart stops beating in my chest. He's here? He's here. My brain can barely function properly after hearing those three words leave Adia's lips. I haven't seen him in three whole weeks. How does he look now? Does he look the same, or has he perhaps even grown a beard? Why am I even thinking about that? I don't even like beards on men. But maybe on him . . . no. *No, Havyn. Stop.*

I'm pulled out of my thoughts when suddenly, I'm moving. Adia's pushing me into the café's bathroom. I'm struck frozen by my own reflection in the mirror. Why do I look like that? My skin is pale, like I've seen a ghost, but my cheeks are flushed, a red colour tinting them.

My body's reactions are strange. They're all over the place, so I'm not even sure of what I'm feeling. Am I scared, nervous, or even . . . happy? I'm not sure. I can't be sure, and even though the warmth blossoming in my chest points to one certain thing, I still struggle to believe in it.

He's here.

"Havyn," a voice cuts into my thoughts. "What are you waiting for? Get undressed."

Undressed? It's only now that I notice Adia stripping out of her clothes, leaving her in merely a lacy bra and a thin panty.

"What? Why?" I stammer, my eyes widening. It's not like I haven't seen Adia naked before and vice versa, but this is all so sudden that all I want to do is look anywhere besides at her.

"Havyn," she snaps, her hands grasping my arms firmly. "Calm down."

I nod, taking a deep breath in and releasing it.

"Look, Alessandro is out there right now, and if he sees you in these tacky clothes, he'll be suspicious. So we're going to swap clothes, and you'll make a run for it," she explains.

"But why are we swapping clothes if I'm making a run for it?" I ask.

"Because if he sees you as you leave the café, at least he'll see you in my expensive clothes, so he won't be suspicious of us," she says.

I nod. What she says makes sense. But still, I'm nervous. The mere thought of him makes me nervous, so how am I going to be able to get out of the café without collapsing to the ground from wobbly legs?

"I'll take over your shift here, at least until he leaves. Okay?"

I nod and then proceed to slip out of my jeans and hoodie before handing them to her to put on. She hands me her clothes, and I hold them up in the air, scanning my eyes over the articles of clothing. Pink mini-skirt with a matching blazer and a pair of white pumps with nude stockings. So formal. So preppy. So . . . not me.

But I shrug those feelings off, slipping the skirt up my legs and pulling my arms through the sleeves of the white blouse and pink sparkly blazer. I then proceed to pull the nude stockings up my legs before slipping my feet into the pumps. Not even a moment passes before I'm pulled by my arm, and I see Adia's make-up bag in her hands.

"Do we have to do this, too?" I groan, pleading to her with my eyes.

"Adia Hamilton would never be seen with a bare face," is all she says before pulling open the bag and pulling out a range of make-up items, some commonly known ones that I know, such as lipstick and mascara, and some I've never seen before. She sets them all down on the counter behind me and pulls my face up straight before working her *magic* on me.

Luckily, like the night of the date, she keeps the makeup to a minimum by just using blush, concealer, eyeliner, mascara, eyeshadow, and lipstick. It's a lot, in my eyes, and I instinctively feel the need to dunk my face in a pool of water and wash it all off, but I resist the urge, just puckering my lips as she drags a glaze of lip gloss onto my lips, the finishing touch.

"There. That should be good enough," she says, taking a step back from me.

I turn around in my spot, my reflection in the mirror startling me for a moment. Once again, just like that night, I look pretty. Make-up really does wonders for a person's appearance, but it's not enough that it'll make me wear it on a daily basis, though. I like my bare face and feel confident enough in it to not care.

A surprised yelp escapes my lips when I suddenly feel a harsh tug on my hair that releases my thick strands from their confinement and causes them to cascade over my shoulders and down my back. Adia then proceeds to drag a brush through my hair, straightening over the slight natural waves before tying a necklace and bracelet around my neck and wrist.

"There. We're done now," she announces, zipping her make-up bag closed. It's only now that I take a moment to look at her. Her appearance has drastically changed since putting on my clothes, and her face is stripped of its makeup, though she does leave a natural touch of product on it to hide her bare face from the public. "You ready?"

Ready to see Alessandro again? No, and I don't think I ever will be. But I have to get through this situation. Hopefully after this, I'll never have to see him again . . . no, that's a lie.

No, Havyn. All you have to do is remain calm and walk out of

---

the café without even sparing him a single glance, like you don't even know he's there. Do not be tempted to look. Otherwise, you might do something you'll come to regret, especially since he may be married now.

So, putting on a brave face, I nod, saying, "Let's do this."

Adia smiles, grabs my hand, and leads the two of us out of the bathroom.

"I'll take your orders, so all you have to do is just get out of here as quickly as you can," Adia says before wrapping the apron around her waist and disappearing into the kitchen.

Okay. I can do this. I can walk out of here.

Taking a deep breath, I clutch Adia's bag, which we swapped with mine, in between my fingers and start moving. I look straight ahead, not wanting to risk the chance of catching a glimpse of him. Who knows, it might tempt me too much.

Yes, you can do this. Just walk straight. The exit isn't far from here.

And then I hear him. His laugh. And as if in instinct, my head snaps to the source of the sound, my eyes finding the back of his head.

How can one person have such an attractive and appealing backside profile? Before, I couldn't care less, but now . . . it's changed. He's changed me. After just one night. After just a few hours.

Before this, I never had any kind of romantic feelings for someone else. No silly crushes, first love, or anything even remotely close to it. But he's changed that. Now, as I stare at him with probably heart eyes, I feel like rushing over to him, jumping into his arms, and giggling like a little schoolgirl with her first crush. Both are true in my case, though.

But he's not alone. I barely notice the person sitting opposite him at the secluded booth. It's a man, his aura not nearly as intimidating as Alessandro's. He's handsome, with light grey eyes and a mop of blond hair sitting on his head. I can hardly believe two people who are clearly so different sitting together. But they are, and the blond man is the one who made *my* Alessandro laugh.

No, Havyn. Alessandro is not yours. And he never will be.

I'm about to force myself to look away and keep walking, but then I hear them talking.

"So why don't you just go to her if you're so miserable without her?" Alessandro's friend says, taking a sip of his latte. I can't help but come to an abrupt stop. Her? Who's her? The woman he's chosen to wed? His wife?

"You know why I can't, Eddie." Alessandro breathes out, his voice snappy and clipped.

"Yeah, because of your father," Eddie says with an eye roll. "So what? Who cares what your father says? You're the Don. You're the one in charge. If you want this girl, go and get her. Don't let your father's demands influence you."

"I don't know . . ." Alessandro trails off.

"The Alessandro I know goes after what he wants and doesn't give a shit about what other people say, not even his own father," Eddie says, staring at him pointedly. "Fuck your father and his standards, and go get you your girl."

Your girl. Who's that? I can't stop the jealousy that creeps into my body like a disease that will slowly torture me until I eventually die.

Shoving that negative feeling away, I continue my walk to the doors. Fine. If that night meant nothing to him and he's already obsessed with another girl, it's fine. I'll get over it.

I finally make it out of the café, and without any control, I sink down to the ground and choke on a sob.

No, I won't.

Chapter Fifteen: Havyn

D*on't cry.*
Don't you dare cry, Havyn.
You're better than this.

No. No, I'm not. I thought I was. I was until meeting him. Now I'm weak and emotional. Just like every other girl he's probably crossed paths with in his life.

No. No, I'm not. I lift my head from between my knees and wipe away the tears falling from my eyes. I can't be. He liked me because of how I was, not because I was weak and emotional. He liked my defiance and my sort of potty mouth.

But then again, why does that matter now? When he likes someone else now?

I choke up another sob. Is this what heartbreak feels like? I don't like it.

At this moment, the door of the café opens, and my head snaps up at the sound of the bell clinging. My eyes widen when they see the people who have exited the café.

Alessandro and his friend.

I turn my head away immediately, cringing at the brief sting in my head from the sudden movement.

"So?" Eddie prods, both of them coming to a stop, it seems.

No. Go away. Keep moving. Don't stay here. Leave. Leave now.

"Are you going to her now?"

"I haven't made my decision yet," Alessandro says in response. Eddie groans in frustration.

"And why the hell not?" he exclaims.

"You forget, my dear friend. She lied to me," Alessandro

reminds him.

"So what? She didn't do it to hurt you. She just wanted to help her friend. I'd do the same for you," Eddie says. "Look, I know that her lying to you doesn't really bother you that much, especially since you know her reason for it. What's really going on here? And don't you dare lie to me. I know you like the back of my hand."

Alessandro sighs. "I don't know. I've spent the last three weeks wanting nothing more than to go to her . . . than to be with her and touch her and kiss her. But now that I feel like I can, I'm hesitant."

Three weeks? Three weeks . . . that's how long it's been since our date. No way . . . is he talking about me? But he's saying that this girl lied to him to help her friend. That sounds like me. Oh my, does he know who I really am? And he still wants me?

The mere thought is unfathomable. What if it's not me they're talking about? What if my desperate desire to be acknowledged by him again is clouding my judgment and deluding me into thinking that he actually wants me?

"Have your feelings for her changed suddenly?" Eddie asks, his voice hesitant.

"No," Alessandro exclaims. "They haven't. It's just . . . what if she . . . doesn't want me?"

"Why wouldn't she want you? From what you've told me of your date with her, she seemed pretty into you, too," Eddie notes.

"But it's been three weeks since then, since I promised to come to her again," he says. *Oh my. It really is me. He's talking about me!* "What if she thinks that I never came for her because my feelings changed or because I lied to her about my interest in her? What if she's found someone else during this time?"

No. I haven't. There can't be anyone else. Not when my mind is filled with you. Only you.

"Dude!" Eddie exclaims. "Who cares? So what if she found

someone else? You can just steal her from him. It's completely within your abilities."

"And if he already fucked her?" Alessandro questions, a certain bite to his voice that makes even me flinch on the ground.

"Then kill him," Eddie says, as if it's just *that* simple. I guess it is for someone like Alessandro. I silently wonder if he's done something like that before—stolen a woman from another man or killed another man for touching someone he wants.

I remember what he said to me that night. That he considers me his. Does he still? Would it bother him if I let someone else touch me, kiss me, and sleep with me before him? It sounds like it does, and that alone has a certain heat creeping in between my legs. Why do I find that sexy? Why does it make me want him to claim me right here, on this sidewalk?

I feel as ashamed of what I feel as I feel shameless. I wasn't aware that it was possible to feel both emotions at the same time.

"I'll call my people to track her exact location down," Alessandro announces to his friend.

Track my location? But I'm right here. I'm right here, yet as much as I want to feel his arms around me once more, I can't bring my legs to move. I'm rooted in this spot.

Should I call out to him? Would he even hear me? Would he be angry that I've just eavesdropped on his entire conversation with his friend? He seems like someone who values privacy, and I just invaded his by not making my presence known and instead listening to his conversation. But the conversation was about me, so didn't I deserve to know? I think so. Would he think so, too? I doubt it.

"Ms. Hamilton?" a familiar voice calls out, pulling me out of my thoughts. I know that voice. Where do I know this voice from . . . oh no. My eyes widen in horror when I look up and see the middle-aged man standing before me. Alessandro's driver.

"*Amore mio?*" another familiar voice calls out merely seconds later. Alessandro's. My head snaps to the side, my wide eyes meeting Alessandro's narrowed ones. Oh no. I've been caught.

"*Amore mio?*" Eddie repeats from beside Alessandro. Then his eyes flutter to me. "So you must be the famous girl who's managed to steal my best friend's heart."

Just like the first time I was caught eavesdropping by Alessandro, I raise my hand in the air and smile awkwardly.

"Hi."

CHAPTER SIXTEEN: HAVYN

The whole outfit-swapping thing was useless.

Because here I am, under the scrutinising eyes of Alessandro, his friend, and his driver. And two of them know who I really am. That I'm Havyn Miller, not Adia Hamilton.

"What are you doing here?" Eddie's the first one to speak, breaking the tense silence that surrounds us.

"I work here," I simply say, pointing my thumb in the direction of the café.

"Ms. Hamilton, why don't you get off the ground?" the driver suggests, taking a step toward me and holding out his hand to me while leaning closer to me. Within a single moment, his hand is swatted away by another. Alessandro's. I stare up at him with wide eyes. He hasn't said another word yet to me or to anyone else. But now he doesn't want his driver helping me? Even his driver can't touch me? What's this caveman behaviour, and why do I like it?

"Hey. Isn't that Alessandro Romano?"

"The Italian mafia Don?"

Whispers start to fill the air around us, and I can't help but feel uncomfortable as everyone's stares alternate between Alessandro and me. I can imagine what must be going through their heads right now. What's Alessandro doing in public with a girl? Adia's clothes might be enough to shield my true identity, but I know it does nothing to hide the fright on my face. This is overwhelming.

"*Amore mio*," I hear Alessandro call out. My eyes snap back to his. He's now right in front of me, leaning on his feet to keep him above the ground as he bends down before me.

"*Amore mio?*"

"Did he just call her *his love*?"

Alessandro reaches out, his hand coming to cup my face, and I can't help but lean into his gentle touch. He lets me revel in the feeling for a brief moment before suddenly, his one arm is picking me up from beneath my legs, and the other wraps around my lower back as he picks me up bridal style.

Gasps erupt from around us. I catch sight of Adia's shocked face before a hand directs my head into Alessandro's neck, hiding me from everyone's stares. His natural body scent invades my senses, smelling like apples and cinnamon. He smells unbelievably nice.

"What the hell is going on here?" a familiar voice yells out. Adia's.

Alessandro's grip on me tightens. "Ms. Hamilton."

"You . . . you know who I am?" Adia stutters out, and when I try to move my head to look at her, Alessandro pushes it further into his neck.

"Is it really such a shock that *I* knew of the ruse you pulled?" he questions.

"Well, where are you taking my best friend?" she demands, but even I can pick up on the tremble in her voice. She's just putting up a brave front, but she's terrified of him and of what he may do to her. Or even to me.

"That's none of your business." he snaps.

"It is when you might hurt her," she persists.

I can only imagine how red her face must be right now. I want to tell her it's okay, that he won't hurt me, even if I can't fully guarantee it myself. It's more hoping than truly knowing.

"I don't hurt what's mine," Alessandro says.

Adia immediately gasps.

Mine. He's calling me that once more. He still considers me his. I can't stop the smile from spreading across my lips at his words. Since when do I like caveman behaviour? I always used to cringe at guys like him, whether it be possessive boyfriends I read about in books or ones I see in real life. But with him, it's different. *He's* different.

Wow. I'm really smitten. I can only hope his feelings for me match mine for him.

I know what usually happens with first loves. It ends up in heartbreak, which leaves you scarred for years after. I'm not looking to go through that.

"Do you . . . do you have feelings for Havyn?" Adia asks, her voice hesitant. I hold my breath as both Adia and I wait for his answer.

"I consider her mine. Is that not enough?" he questions.

I smile softly, unable to stop myself from planting a soft kiss on the base of his neck. He tenses up underneath my mouth, before relaxing, his grip on me tightening.

I remember his words from that night. *"I want to kiss you so badly. But I won't, not until you want me to."*

If we weren't in public right now, I'd make him own up to it, because I most definitely want him to now.

"What about Havyn? Does she have feelings for you, too?" Adia questions.

She's persistent because she cares about me. I've always admired that trait in her, but right now, I just want her to stop talking so that Alessandro can take me far away from here. I'll deal with whatever comes after that later. "Does she? I want to hear her say it herself. Otherwise, I won't let you take her."

There's a few moments of silence before I feel a light brush against my cheek.

"*Amore mio,*" he whispers. He says nothing more. There's nothing more for him to say. And so I do a brave thing by lifting my head out of his neck and turning it so that my eyes meet Adia's. I'm not sure what she sees in my eyes, but she gasps, her eyes becoming wide and her lips parting in shock.

"Havyn," she whispers, disbelief seeping from her voice. "You really . . . why?"

She knows. I don't know what I look like right now, but clearly, my feelings are written all over my face, and she can read them.

I don't answer her question, turning away from her and leaning my head on Alessandro's shoulder again. I've left Adia speechless, and even though guilt pricks at my skin for it, I keep my mouth shut. One day. One day, I'll tell her the truth.

Alessandro takes her silence as an out and gestures to his driver that he'll be leaving now. That *we'll* be leaving now. I don't have it in me to look at Adia one more time before Alessandro climbs into the car with me still in his arms, and the car door closes.

"I'm sorry," I whisper once I feel the car start to move, and silence surrounds us. He doesn't respond, but he doesn't push me out of his hold, so I take that as a good sign.

"Where to, sir?" the driver speaks up.

"My penthouse, Billy," Alessandro answers. Billy, that's the driver's name. I should probably stop referring to him as *the driver* in my mind now that I know.

"Alessandro," I can't help but call out softly.

He doesn't respond.

"Do . . . do you hate me?"

"We'll talk about this in private," he merely says, dismissing my question. My heart sinks, but I try not to let it show. This is my own fault. I lied to him, I deceived him, so he deserves to be angry at me. I only hope that he doesn't hate me. Is it possible to like someone and hate them at the same time? I'm not sure. But I don't say anything else for the rest of the drive. I just keep my head situated comfortably on his shoulder.

I'm not sure how much time has passed, but it feels like a

good amount before we finally come to a stop, and Billy announces, "We're here, sir."

I lift my head and make a move to get off his lap, but Alessandro is quick to pull me back to his chest, startling me. Was I wrong? Is he not angry at me?

"Stay," he says. No, he more like commands it, and surprisingly, I don't mind. I like it in his arms. He opens the car door and climbs out with me. I can't help but look up to see where we are, and I gasp when I see the tall building before us. Is it a skyscraper? Looks like it. Just like his hotel, there's a golden glow that shines through all the windows. It's just another reminder of *how* wealthy he is. So different from me.

No, Havyn. Let's not think about that now, especially when you are in his arms. Since he knows who I really am and is still willing to be in my presence, milk it. Milk him for all the affection and love he's got.

He carries me into the building through the rotating doors and walks through a large lobby before stopping by an elevator and pressing the up button. After a few moments, the elevator doors open, and he steps in before pressing the top-floor button. He did tell Billy to take him to his penthouse.

The elevator ride is silent and quite fast, considering how many floor levels it must travel up before it finally comes to a stop. To my confusion, the doors don't open. It's only when Alessandro leans down slightly and presses his finger to a fingerprint scanner that I notice it. His fingerprint must probably be the only way to get onto the top floor. Within a few seconds after scanning, the elevator doors slide open, revealing the penthouse. The elevator must act as an entrance to the penthouse. *How cool!*

I gasp in awe as he carries me inside, my eyes wide as they scan over everything. At the entrance, there is a living room with cream cotton couches and plush white cushions. Further in is the kitchen with an island and everything. And then lastly, there's a little hallway at the end, probably where his bedroom is. The thought of his bedroom has my cheeks flushing with heat. Why am I so weird? All around him.

And then to add to my embarrassment, in this very moment, my stomach decides to grumble out loud, the loudest it's ever been. Alessandro comes to a stop, and I purse my lips. There it is.

"Are you hungry?" he questions. I nod quite timidly, so unlike my character. He walks to the kitchen and places me on the kitchen island before walking to the refrigerator and pulling it open. This is the first time he's let me go since finding me, and it feels strange to not be in his warm arms.

As I look at the place and then down at my own lap, I can't help but wonder. How many other women did he bring here? Did he bring Aliya here? Probably. They did go out for three whole years, after all. I hate the jealousy that comes along with the thought. Clearly, as a man of his age, he's a lot more experienced than I am. He's seen more, he's been through more, and that definitely extends to the bedroom, too. It's not like I thought he was a virgin. I never thought that. But now, being here in his home has unwanted images flashing in my head. Images of multiple women entering and exiting this place. Beautiful women with long legs, big breasts, and voluptuous figures.

And then I look down at myself. At a height of 5'1 with a body that has no curves whatsoever and breasts that are in between existing and being non-existent, I'm nothing compared to the women he must have been with before. Women. He's been with women, and I'm merely a girl. A high school girl who has nothing to offer him but an average body.

Without even noticing, I blink, and a tear falls from my eye. I move my hand up wipe it away, but I'm not fast enough, because before I can, Alessandro is in front of me, and his hand is around my wrist, stopping my movements. There's a certain seriousness in his eyes as he stares down at me, his eyes a dark green.

"Stop that," he commands. I blink in surprise.

"What?"

"Stop that. Whatever you're doing, stop it," he firmly says.

Stop it? What, degrading myself? I can nod, but how can I stop doing that exactly? I can't, not when I see myself in that specific way. And then suddenly, he tugs me forward so that my bottom is at the edge of the kitchen island, and his thick thighs force my legs open.

My face heats up at our close proximity. He's so close, not just his face, but the rest of his body, too. I can feel him, including *that* part of him, pressing firmly against my pelvis. I try not to squirm and pull away from him because then he will know what he does to me. I wonder if he can feel the heat between my legs? I'm sure he can, especially since I'm wearing a short skirt with nothing but thin stockings underneath. Why don't I ask him to move?

"What . . . what are you doing?" I stammer out. I can only imagine how red I must be right now.

"What does it look like I'm doing?" he questions, raising an eyebrow at me. I gulp. "What? Are you nervous?"

Gulp. Swallow.

"Are you nervous because you like being this close to me?" he questions, his tone teasing. He knows, so why does he bother asking? No, he's getting a high from this, watching me blush and squirm when he's barely even touching me.

He leans down to slip off my pumps, his gaze not leaving mine once as he does. He drops the shoes to the floor with a soft plat, and then his hands move up again, coming to rest on my hips. There's so much fabric between his hands and my skin right now, but my skin still feels like it's on fire.

"It's a little hot in here, isn't it?" he murmurs, his hands trailing up my arms until it stops at the top of the blazer I'm wearing. "Why don't we get rid of this, huh?"

No. No. This is too much, is what my brain screams, but despite that, I let him pull the blazer down my arms before he carelessly tosses it aside. I can't help but take a quick glance at it as it lies completely abandoned on the floor. I'm sure that item alone costs more than my monthly salary at the café. Is it bad that even in this situation, I want to pick it up, fold it up, and place it neatly on a clean surface?

Alessandro seems to notice that I'm distracted, because his fingers grip my chin, forcing my gaze to meet his. "Focus on me. Only me."

I gulp but nod anyway.

"What do you want?" he murmurs, his question surprising me.

"What do you mean?" I can't help but ask in surprise.

"Whatever you want to do. Just name it, and I'll fulfil your wants," he says.

Whatever I want to do? Does he mean in general, or . . . sexually? What am I even thinking? In a situation this heated, of course he means sexually. Only an idiot like me would be dumb and say something stupid that would ultimately break the moment. The question is, do I want to, or do I want something else? Something more? He did say whatever I want, but even though my body sizzles with desire for him, I want to take this slow. In this aspect of life, I'm about just as inexperienced as a newborn baby. Heck, I haven't even had my first kiss yet.

And then I realise that maybe that's where I can start. I can ask him to kiss me. But with a man like him, as passionate and raw as he is, would it stop with just a kiss? What if his hands wander? What if he tries to feel me up, or worse, he tries to take me back to his bed with him? As much as I want him, I know that right now, I'm not ready for *that* yet. Heck, I won't be able to handle more. I feel like with just one look from him at the right place, I'll combust right in his arms.

My eyes lift to his. This entire time that I've spent thinking, he's remained quiet. I quickly realise I want him to touch me, perhaps even kiss me in more than one place, but there's still something hanging in the air. I'd asked him if he hates me, and he said we would talk in private. Is it really a good idea to pursue something this intimate, even just a kiss, before talking things out?

I don't want to believe it, but a part of me fears that after I give a part of myself to him, he'll kick me out and laugh in my face for being so naïve into thinking he actually feels something for me after I lied to him.

"It's okay," he suddenly says, tearing through my negative thoughts. He cups my cheek with his hand. "Everything's okay."

Everything's okay. I'm not sure what exactly everything that he's referring to is, but I nod, allowing that to wash away my worries for now, just for this single moment.

My hands lift, and I hesitantly wrap my arms around his neck. His eyes don't leave mine, even as I try to look away before ultimately meeting his intense gaze once more. And then I say words I thought I'd never utter in my lifetime.

"I want you to touch me."

CHAPTER SEVENTEEN: HAVYN

His touch is hot on my skin.

First, he trails his fingers from my cheek down my neck, until he reaches the top of the blouse I'm wearing. He pinches the fabric in between his fingers, staring at it as though it is in the way. In a sense, I guess it is. I can ease his frustration. I can tell him to take off my blouse, but the weight of that is heavy . . . heavier than I think I can handle right now. So I don't, keeping my lips sealed shut.

"Would you mind if I take your stockings off?" he requests, his eyes fluttering to mine. I'm surprised by his sudden request. It's not like I wasn't expecting him to eventually take my stockings off, maybe even rip them off, but him actually asking me if I'm okay with him doing so? That's what surprises me. He seems like a man who would do whatever he wants without asking for permission. Was I wrong about him, or is he being this gentle and nice with me because he knows of my inexperience? The mere thought of him knowing of my innocence has me blushing and looking away from him.

Like an ugly disease, that brings back what Aubrey said at the party. He likes defiling virgins. He gets a kick out of it. I flinch at the mere thought. What if that's all he wants from me? I mean, what better revenge than making me believe he truly feels something for me and taking my virginity before throwing me away?

I shake my head. Why am I thinking this way? Are my insecurities so major that even in this moment, I can't help but think only of the bad? I can barely focus on how gentle his touch is, and how good it feels. All I can focus on is the bad. The bad that I don't even know is true. I'm very good at deluding myself into believing things that aren't even true. I'm scared that that's what's happening right now.

"Havyn," Alessandro calls out, my heart stopping in my chest. Havyn, he's called me by my real name for the first time. It feels good. It feels like he's acknowledging *me* and not a façade I spent hours building. It feels *real*.

"I'm sorry," I whisper, my eyes avoiding his as I feel tears prick at my skin once more. "I'm a mess."

"You're not a mess," he says, lifting my head with his fingers.

I shake my head at his words. Yes, I am. Very much so. "Does it bother you that much?"

"I just want to know if you hate me," I admit, staring up at him with teary eyes.

His hand cups the side of my face, his thumb wiping away a tear as it falls. "I don't hate you," he says, leaning forward to nuzzle his nose against mine. "I like you too much to ever hate you."

"But you're angry at me?" I ask.

"Mm." He hums. "I was very angry at first. But then I realised, why should I spend all my time being angry when I can have you by my side every day, in my arms, in my bed? It wasn't worth it."

He's being honest. I can hear it in his voice. He seems like a man who hardly ever speaks openly about his feelings, and I have to admit, this feels nice. It's also extremely relieving. To know that he doesn't hate me. He can still be a little angry. That's okay. As long as he doesn't hate me, I can deal with it.

For the first time in ages, a real smile spreads across my face. His eyes widen slightly, and he blinks out of it. I lean forward, my face nearing his. I turn my head to the side, pressing my lips to his cheek. The lipstick Adia put on me leaves an imprint on his cheek, and I kind of like it. It feels like I'm claiming him as mine, as naïve as that may be.

"You told me you wouldn't kiss me until I want you to," I murmur into his ear. He hums in recognition of this. And then I lean back slightly so that I can look at him in the eyes. "Well, I kind of want you to kiss me now."

"Oh really?" he teases. I nod. "Where?"

"Anywhere. Everywhere," I say before thinking. That might be a bit much for right now.

"Really? How about here?" he murmurs, his lips meeting my neck. "Or here?" He places wet kisses down my throat, and I have to stop myself from giggling. That's ticklish. "Or maybe even here?"

I gasp when his fingers trail up my thighs and graze against the most sensitive part of my body. He pulls his hand away quickly, and I have to force myself not to bring it back and make him touch it properly this time. Not now. Not yet.

"How about here?" I say, blinking innocently up at him as I tap my lips with my finger. His gaze travels down, landing on my lips, and desire flashes in his eyes.

"You sure?" he murmurs. "Because once I claim those lips, I won't let anyone else taste them ever again."

I don't bother telling him that he'll be the first. I just smile up at him. He leans forward, and my eyes flutter closed in anticipation. Then I feel it, the brush of his lips against mine, before he pulls away. My eyes snap open, and I glare at him. What was that? Is he just playing with me?

"What's with that pout, my love?" he teases, pulling me even closer. I didn't know we could get any closer.

"You're not funny," I snap, trying my best to glare at him, but he's hardly affected. He just remains amused. "You know what? It's fine. If you don't want to kiss me then—"

"Shh." He shushes me, placing a finger on my lips. "You want to take things slow, don't you? That's why you won't let me touch you where you ache the most."

How does he know?

"Trust me, *amore mio*. I'm trying my best not to rip off all your clothes and take you against the kitchen island right now."

I gasp at his dirty mouth. He really lacks a filter.

"So don't tempt me."

"Will just a kiss tempt you into sleeping with me?" I tease.

He smirks in response, devilishly. "Oh, you have no idea," he says, pressing himself against me.

I gasp. He's big and *hard*.

"How can you be hard already? We haven't even done anything," I blurt out, my eyes widening once I realise what has just left my mouth.

He smiles. "Just having you propped on this kitchen island with your legs spread for me does wicked things to me," he admits, and I can't help but wonder. Does this happen with other women, too? Was he like this with other women, too? I want to think I'm special, but I can't be certain. My mood deflates, and he quickly notices. "What's wrong now?"

"Nothing," I lie, looking away from him. "I'm just no longer in the mood."

I push him away, only being able to because he looks so surprised and too confused to even try and keep me in place. I then slip off the kitchen island before walking over to where the blazer lies, pick it up, and slip into it. I do the same with the pumps, and then he's turning to me, staring down at my outfit with great displeasure. Of course he hates that I'm fully covered again, even with how short this skirt is on its own.

"Why?" he questions, staring down at me.

"No reason." I shrug. "I just don't want to anymore."

He stares down at me with narrowed eyes, like he doesn't understand. I don't understand either. One moment, I was *seriously* considering ditching my previous reservations and letting him take me to his bed, and the next, all the desire I had for him to do so seeped from my body, leaving nothing but a cold, empty feeling behind.

"No," he says, taking a step toward me. It's only now that I'm actually standing on my own feet in front of him that I notice the height difference between us. Before, on the date, I was wearing heels, so it didn't seem that big, but now that I'm in flat shoes, it's really prominent. Wow, he's really tall. "Something happened. One doesn't just lose all desire to do something like that. So tell me, and don't even think about lying to me."

I flinch at his tone. Of course, he's still sensitive about me lying to him in the first place.

"I'm not lying. It just happens to me . . . sometimes." Okay, so maybe I *am* lying, but it's not like I can just tell him about all my insecurities concerning him and his past with others of my gender.

"I don't believe you," he says.

"Well, how would you know? You don't even know me," I exclaim, and even though it hurts to admit, it's true. We know almost nothing about each other, a fact that I was happy enough to ignore while his hands were on me, but now that we have some space between us, I can't anymore. And then my tone simmers down. "I don't even know what I'm doing here."

His gaze softens a little, and he takes another step towards me, but I take one back in return.

"Please. Don't come any closer," I say, holding my hand up in the air. I feel like I want to cry. What's wrong with me? Why am I so emotional and confused today?

"*Amore mio,*" he calls out.

"No," I firmly say. "Don't call me that. It's because you called me that that I gave in like I did. I shouldn't have come here with you. I should have resisted. I should have just stayed with Adia back at the café. I don't know what I was thinking."

"Listen—"

"No!" I cut him off, starting to pace around the room and muttering to myself. "What's wrong with me? Why did I get myself involved with a mafia Don? Why did I get my emotions mixed up in all of this? Why did I—"

Suddenly, I'm spun around, my eyes instinctively moving to meet his.

"Stop rambling. Talk to me," he says.

"I need to go," I blurt out. "I can't be here. I have things I need to do. I have work. I have school."

At this point, I'm freaking out, and I can see by the look in his eyes that he's starting to get frustrated with me, and I can't expect anything less from him. I'm pretty sure none of his other lovers were so much work, so of course he's getting fed up with me. God, why did I come here with him? I'm so stupid.

"Havyn," he snaps, his voice loud and booming over my thoughts. "I'm only going to say this once. You need to calm the fuck down, and you need to do it now."

I flinch at his harsh words.

"Listen, I've been patient with you. You were mature enough that night three weeks ago for me to be able to overlook the fact that you're a fucking child, but if you continue to act this way, I might have to change my mind," he snaps. Tears prick at my eyes.

"Why are you being so mean all of a sudden?" I whimper.

He's hardly bothered. "Because I don't have a lot of patience with people, and right now, you're getting on my last nerve. You're right. You could have resisted back there and not come here with me, but you decided to let me bring you here, so if you want to do adult things, you're going to have to act like an adult and not throw a tantrum when something happens."

Tantrum? Was I just throwing a tantrum?

"So you have two choices now," he says. "Either you put on your big girl panties, or you get out."

My heart hurts. I like him, and I thought he liked me, too, so why is he being so mean to me?

Tears threaten to fall, but I hold them back, somehow, and force a determined expression on my face.

"Fine," I say, walking past him to the elevator and pressing the button. When the doors open, I step inside and press the ground floor button.

When I look up, he's still standing there, now staring at me in the elevator, about to leave. He's a jerk, but a part of me still wishes that he would change his mind, stop me from leaving, and apologize for treating me that way. But I know he won't. That would make him seem weak, and that's the last thing he, a mafia Don, wants to come off as. He's strong, a man, and I'm just another weak girl he lured into his home.

But I'm getting out now, and I'm never coming back.

Chapter Eighteen: Alessandro

I fucked up.
I fucked up badly.

I hurt *her*. I hurt the person who I haven't gotten off my mind for almost a month. I finally saw her, and I hurt her. I hurt her a lot. I can try and lie to myself to make myself feel better, but I can't. No, I *won't*. The pain on her face, the tears in her eyes, are burned into my mind. It's barely been 24 hours since she walked out of my apartment, and I'm already missing her like crazy.

I touched her. I had my fingers against her most private part, even though it was merely for a second. She was turned on. I could feel it even through the material that separated her from my fingers. I was too, but I held back. I didn't want to scare her. She was so hot, but then the next moment, she was so cold, pushing me away and putting on the clothes I took off her.

The way she looked while doing that, she looked so frazzled, confused, and scared, even. I really shouldn't have reacted the way I did, especially after I tried so hard not to do anything that would scare her off, but when she didn't listen to me, I just lost it. Maybe it's because I'm used to everyone *always* listening to me. Even my previous lovers. They treated me like I owned them, like they were inferior to me, and I think that was the thing I liked the most about them, that they didn't question me or anything I said or did.

But Havyn . . . she's different. And I don't like that. I don't like that she has a voice of her own. I don't like that she zones off so much and doesn't always pay attention to me. I don't like that she can talk back to me and defy me.

Honestly, when I gave her that ultimatum, I thought, no, I expected her to submit to me and my demand for her to stop acting like a child, but she didn't. Instead, she walked out. No one's ever walked out on me before. For a moment, I was angry at her for walking out on me, but then, as time passed by, my anger shifted from her towards myself. I was angry at myself. I still am. Angry that I yelled at her. Angry that I was so rude to her. Angry that I swore at her. Angry that I hurt her. Angry that I made her cry. Angry that I didn't stop her when I had the chance.

And like the bastard that I am, even after coming to the realization, I haven't gone to find her. No, instead, I sit here in my office, drowning myself in paperwork that could have been done later. I'm stuck, though. Every time I sign a document or read through shipment papers, I see her face. I'm not sure why, since she has no place in my mind right now, but there she is.

"Dude," a vacant voice calls out. Then again. And again. "Alessandro! Havyn was kidnapped!"

I'm up from my seat instantly.

"Who dared take her?" I growl, my eyebrows furrowing in confusion when I see my best friend holding his fist to his mouth, the expression on his face telling me that he's dying to burst out laughing. "What the hell?"

"I doubted it would work. But damn, you've got it bad," he says through choked-up chuckles.

"What the hell is wrong with you, Edward?" I growl, using his full name to show him that I'm not impressed with him as I collapse back into my chair.

"Why? Were you scared for a second?" he teases.

I don't respond because, for a second, I was. I was scared. What the hell is up with that? What the hell is up with me? I barely know the girl. We've only met twice, so why the hell do I care what happens to her?

"What do you want?" I question, avoiding having to answer him by changing the subject. He raises an eyebrow at me, clearly picking up on my attempt, but he shrugs nonetheless, falling into the seat opposite me quite dramatically.

"Just missed you," he says.

"Don't bullshit me. Why are you really here?" I question, crossing my arms as I stare at him with a quirked eyebrow.

"Fine," he says in defeat, acting like I fought him for it. "You left with Ms Miller. How'd that go? You two get freaky in the sheets?"

The way he wiggles his eyebrows at me has anger creeping into me. *No, Alessandro. Don't take your anger out on someone else.*

"No," I growl, displeased at the fact that *nothing* happened between us. Yes, I touched her, but barely. I didn't even get to kiss her, taste her. She pulled away before that. I still can't help but wonder. She was so into it, into me, so why did she suddenly become so cold? She told me that she just wasn't into it anymore, but I don't believe that. I saw her zone out seconds before that. Something happened in her brain. What in the world was she thinking about?

"Shame. You must be feeling so blue right now, more than one part of you," Eddie says, pouting. It's not sincere, though. He's teasing me for not getting laid.

"Sometimes I really hate you," I say, my tone serious. He merely shakes his head with a laugh.

"No, you don't. You don't hate me. You hate that I'm right," he says as a matter of fact. And once again, he's right. "So? What happened? The Alessandro I know would never let a woman he likes out of his sight before he beds her."

"She ran from me," I admit softly, honestly embarrassed to admit it. I expect him to burst out laughing, tease me or do something unhelpful, but instead, his eyes soften.

"Why did she run?" he asks.

"I yelled at her. Pissed her off," I say. He nods. He understands. This is why I like Eddie. This is why he's my best friend. He understands me, twisted ways and all.

"And now what? You're done with her since she walked out on you?" he asks.

He knows me so well. If it was any other woman, I'd have put a bullet between her eyes by now, but this is Havyn. She's different.

My silence must speak a thousand words, because not even a minute later, Eddie shakes his head. "I hate to say it, my friend," he starts, sending a pitiful look my way before continuing. "You're screwed."

I am. I know I am.

Shit. I need to go to her.

CHAPTER NINETEEN: HAVYN

What am I doing?

The reality of my decision weighs on me as I stand in front of my old apartment building, Randy's building. Why did I think coming here was a good idea? Oh, right, because I wanted to forget about what happened with Alessandro, and I knew that it wouldn't take any more than a single word to make Randy give me some of his goods. Throughout the two years I lived here, he always wanted me to try out drugs with the rest of his friends, but I always refused. But now, I guess his wish is about to come true.

I ignore the bad feeling in my stomach that tells me I really shouldn't be here and walk up to the building, ascending the stairs and passing my old apartment to Randy's apartment at the end. With one knock on the door, the door flies open, and a woman appears before my eyes. She's clearly a prostitute, barely wearing anything to cover her private parts and with a bottle of vodka in her hand.

"Can I help you?" she questions, raising an unimpressed eyebrow at me.

"I'm here to see Randy," I say.

"He's busy," she says, about to close the door on me, but I take a step forward.

"Just tell him Miller is here," I confidently say. Why am I so confident? I have no idea. I'm not even sure Randy wants to see me after he kicked me out. I know he's fed up with me, but hopefully, he still likes me enough to see me.

She hesitates in the doorway for a few moments before

turning around and walking back into the apartment. Not much time passes before she returns. "Come in."

I ignore the jealousy evident in her voice and on her face as she invites me in. These prostitutes get so jealous, like they don't sleep with multiple other men on a daily basis.

There's an awful stench of weed and sweat lingering in the air as I walk in, but I'm used to it. My apartment used to smell like this almost five days throughout the week when I lived here. When I reach the living room, I find Randy and a couple of his friends sitting on the couches with Randy in the centre on the one-person couch, smoking weed, the others each with a bottle of alcohol in their hands.

"Well, if it isn't my favourite pretty girl," Randy announces, his eyes twinkling as he stares up at me. His friends smile at me. I hate the way they stare at me like they're undressing me with their eyes. I have no doubt they are. "What brings you to my humble abode, Havyn?"

I flinch. He's never called me by my name before. He always called me by my last name, Miller.

No, I shouldn't react this way. I should stick it all up and accept it with a smile.

"I just missed you." A lie that comes to me easily.

"You? Missed me?" He chuckles, and I nod. "Well, isn't this a surprise? But I'm glad, because I missed you, too. Why don't you come over here to Daddy, huh?"

I try not to visibly show my disgust at his choice of words, swallowing it down and walking over to him. The moment I'm within his reach, he grabs my arm and tugs me down onto his lap. I try not to recoil at his touch.

"Would you like a drink, baby?" he murmurs, his voice is sickly sweet. A drink. I've never drunken alcohol before, partially because I'm underage but mainly because I didn't want to be under the influence around them. But then again, isn't this why I came here in the first place?

And so, albeit hesitantly, I nod, swallowing my fears. He smiles, leaning forward to grab a beer from the table. It's warm when he hands it to me, but I crack open the top anyway, bringing it to my lips and taking a large gulp before I can even think of talking myself out of it. I try not to throw up at the strange taste. It's bitter, and it makes my throat dry up.

"And?" Randy asks, staring expectantly at me.

"It's . . . nice," I say, forcing a smile onto my face. He smiles, his fingers trailing up and down my arm.

"Anything else you want? I'll give you everything, baby," he says, a glint of something in his eyes. He's trying to get me drunk or high. He knows I won't let him do anything to me otherwise, but even though everything in me tells me to get up and get out of here right now, I remain seated.

"I've always wanted to try weed," I say, unsure of how to word my sentence in a way that doesn't make me sound as much of an amateur as I am.

"Richard, bring me the goods," Randy instructs, and one of his friends gets up and disappears into the kitchen.

Minutes later, he appears with a small packet in his hand. The packet is filled with a pure white powder. *Cocaine.* He hands it to Randy. "Sorry. We just finished all the weed. So all I have for you right now is this."

"That'll do," I say, eagerly taking the packet from him. This is it. This will make me forget. Will I regret doing this? Probably, but right now, I couldn't care less. I just want to forget, even for merely a single moment. I can deal with the consequences and regrets later.

Pulling open the packet, I press my face into the opening and sniffing. It doesn't smell like anything, necessarily.

The rest of it is a blur, and before I even know it, tears are streaming down my face and someone bursts through the door. My heart is stuttering in my chest when I see who it is.

Alessandro.

CHAPTER TWENTY: ALESSANDRO

I'm going to kill this motherfucker.

I can barely believe what I'm seeing. Havyn, *my* Havyn is sitting on some middle-aged bastard's lap with his hand up her skirt. She stares up at me with tears in her eyes, and I feel the rage in me explode.

Before I even realise it, I'm right in front of him, ripping her away from him and connecting my fist with his face. Gasps of shock erupt in the room, but I can hardly care, pummelling the bastard's face in with my fist. Maybe he begs me to stop, but I can't be sure.

All I see is red.

"Dude, stop!" Eddie's voice fills my ears, and then I'm pulled away from the bastard. I struggle against the grip.

"Alessandro!"

I relax slightly.

"Alessandro, she needs you," Eddie says, and my eyes widen. I pull myself away from him and turn around, my focus landing on *her*. She's on the ground, leaning against the wall with her knees against her chest, tears streaming down her face as she clutches her shoulder. Oh no, did I hurt her?

I didn't even think about possibly hurting her earlier. I just wanted her away from him. I approach her slowly, especially when I hear the whimpers escaping her lips. I don't pay any more attention to anyone or anything besides her. I trust Eddie will deal with everything else.

"Havyn," I call out softly, a sting going through my heart when she whimpers in fear. "*Amore mio.*"

My pet name for her does the trick. Her head slowly lifts, and her eyes hesitantly meet mine. She looks so scared and unsure. God, that hurts.

"It's okay," I say as I fall to my knees in front of her. Her lips tremble, and another tear falls.

"Alessandro." She whimpers, her eyes uncertain as she stares at me.

"It's okay," I say, grabbing her arms and pulling her towards me. I gather her fragile form in my arms, stroking her skin. "I'm sorry. I'm so sorry, my love."

This is all my fault. If I hadn't yelled at her, if I hadn't hurt her, she wouldn't have ended up here. I try not to let the fact that that bastard touched her before I did bother me, especially with how fragile she is right now. I can take out my anger on him later. Later when she isn't so scared.

My guys come filtering into the apartment, already ready to clean up whatever mess they know I can make. They're lucky I only beat up one guy today because usually, I make a whole mess, bodies piling on top of one another. I once massacred a whole adult family.

"Havyn, *amore mio*," I softly call her, trying not to scare her. "We have to go now."

It's not like I'm scared of people seeing this entire scene nor of the police that will probably come piling up the street. I'm more worried about *her*. I don't want her to be exposed to that. I also don't want any men to see her like this, tears ruining her make-up and a skirt that barely covers her thighs.

Luckily for me, she agrees quite easily. She must be tired of fighting.

So I gather her in my arms, lifting her up into the air. Like the possessive bastard I am, my one hand grips the hem of her skirt, pulling it as far down as it can go without exposing her back. I carry her out of the building and carefully get into the car with her still in my arms, just like earlier today.

100

Havyn's breaths are steady and low against my skin, and her eyes are closed, her fingers gripping the material of my shirt tightly, as if she trusts me. Maybe she does, even if it's just for now. I'll protect her. To the end. As long as I'm here, no one will touch her. I won't let them.

Ever.

Chapter Twenty-one: Havyn

I'm warm.

Too warm.

There are two arms around me, securing me into a hard yet soft chest. I try to wiggle my body, but a sudden groan from under me has me freezing.

"What do you want, *amore mio*?" a husky voice questions, sleep lacing it.

"Uhm . . . can you please let go of me?" I whisper, my cheeks warming up.

He groans. "No. Let's lay here for a couple more minutes."

My cheeks get warmer. He's not going to move unless I tell him, but how can I tell him without wanting to die from embarrassment?

"Uhm . . . I kind of have to . . ." I trail off. The words won't come out of my mouth.

"What is it that you want to say, my love?" he murmurs lowly.

"I have to pee," I blurt out, my eyes closing tightly shut after my admission. There's silence, and for a few moments, I think that maybe he's going to laugh at me, or worse, call me a child again, even though everyone, including adults, have to pee. It's natural. But then he lifts his arm off me, and without a second thought, I jump up from the bed, stopping for a moment when my feet land on the floor, and I look around.

I'm in a big master bedroom. It's dark, though. Grey curtains cover the windows, allowing no light to filter in. I don't pay much attention to the finer details, though, the pressure between my legs becoming much more apparent, and when my eyes land on a door inside of the room, opposite the bed, I rush to it, pull it open and walk in.

I quickly relieve myself, relaxation washing over me now that I don't feel that hot pressure anymore. The bathroom is fancy, though, with marble detailing and the décor screaming masculinity. The shower is big, too, looking like it can fit at least ten of me in it, closed by merely a glass door. The moveable showerhead stares at me, and I cringe. I know what people do with those. But can guys use it, too? I don't think so. Next to the shower is a pearly white bathtub that looks like a jacuzzi on its own. I'm surprised when I see the bath salts and bubble bath sitting on the side of it. I never thought a guy like Alessandro would like something like that. No, I never thought anything, at least not this close to home. I never allowed myself to.

And then I look in the mirror. My eyes widen in horror. I was too busy trying to relieve myself to notice myself. My hair is loose in its natural waves and everything, but that's not what shocked me. My face has been stripped of all the makeup Adia put on me, and I'm standing in merely a thin white shirt that stops a few inches above my knees, and the first two buttons of the shirt are unbuttoned, leaving a bit of my cleavage exposed. Luckily, when I look inside the shirt, I see that I still have my underwear on. Thank God.

But still, did Alessandro undress me? Himself? My face warms at the thought. That means he saw me in only my underwear. That's embarrassing.

Great. Now I never want to come out of this bathroom. But I have to eventually. Otherwise, Alessandro will come for me. He might even knock the door down to get to me. I wouldn't put it past him. I'm not sure how much time passes by before I'm finally able to put on a brave face and walk out of the bathroom. However, what I see has all the braveness melting from my face.

Alessandro lies in bed on his stomach, the grey sheets covering just his lower half, leaving his entire back exposed. His hair is messy, splaying onto the pillow he lays on. From here, I can see a tattoo in the centre of his back. It's a huge flower that sprouts from the inner crevice of his back, and the petals trail all the way out, causing the tattoo to cover most of his back.

I've never found tattoos on men attractive, but now that I'm seeing him with them, I'm rethinking it, because he just looks so hot to me right now. Is this legal? Probably not. But I'm the younger one in this, so I'm allowed to thirst over him, an older mafia Don.

Can he feel me staring at him? Does he know that I'm basically drooling over him right now?

What do I do? Do I get back into bed with him, or do I just awkwardly stand here until he decides to eventually get up.

"Come back to bed, a*more mio*," he murmurs without even bothering to lift his head. I hesitate, tapping my fingers against my thigh. "Don't make me come get you."

The warning in his voice has me rushing to the bed and plopping onto the bed next to him. Now it's awkward. What do I do? Just lie here?

"*Amore mio*," he calls out, and when I turn my head to him, he's already staring at me. He rolls over onto his side and lifts his one arm. "Come here, baby."

Baby. When Randy called me that, I was disgusted, but for some reason, being called that by Alessandro feels nice. Like he cares about me. But maybe I'm just being naïve. But either way, I scoot closer to him, and once I'm within arm's reach, his arm wraps around my waist, and he pulls me flush against his chest, causing my breath to hitch at our sudden closeness.

"How was the pee?" he teases, an easy smile coming to his face. My face flushed, and in response, his smile widens, a pair of dimples appearing in his cheeks. Wow, that's adorable.

I want to poke them.

Without even realising it, I jut out my finger, and it lands right in his dimple. He blinks in surprise before a soft expression overtakes his face. The way he looks at me, it makes my heart flutter.

I want to kiss him.

And before I realise it, I'm leaning forward. His eyes flash with surprise before they flicker down to my lips, and he licks his own. He wants to kiss me, too. That has desire shooting right through me.

Maybe, just maybe, he wants me as much as I want him.

"*Amore mio,*" he murmurs, his voice so thick with desire that it causes my underwear to dampen.

And then, as if he can no longer control himself, his fingers thread through my hair, and he pulls my mouth down to meet his.

Chapter Twenty-two: Havyn

I gasp.

His lips are so soft, but they press hard against mine, his tongue flicking across my lower lip. The way he kisses me, it's as if he wants to claim me. Then suddenly, his hands are on my hips, and he's pulling me on top of him so that my body straddles his. His hands travel up my body, pulling the shirt up in the process. My hands delve into his hair as I press my lips firmer against his, all my nervousness washing away with every flick of his tongue.

This is my first kiss, and it's definitely not what I expected it to be. It's not like I pictured some fairy-tale-like kiss, but I never thought it would be like this, so hot and heavy and filled with desire. I thought my first kiss would be slow and that I would be coaxed into it somehow, but he's not leading me into anything. If anything, he's throwing me in the deep end, into a wild sea, and expects me to already know how to swim.

I don't hate it, though.

Alessandro's fingers trail underneath the shirt I'm wearing, sliding over my bottom slowly. Then he suddenly pulls at the hem of my underwear and lets go, causing it to slap against my skin, and I gasp in surprise. He smiles into the kiss. He's teasing me, I quickly realise. And then he gets bolder, biting my lower lip and coaxing me to open my mouth so that he can slip his tongue inside.

When his tongue touches mine, my legs tremble. I've seen people tongue kiss one another before, but it always seemed so sloppy and with too much sharing of saliva that I never cared to do it myself. But this, this is different. If anything, I want to trap his tongue inside my mouth.

He tastes so sweet, like a juicy fruit I just want to sink my teeth into. It's strange, considering the fact that he just woke up. I wonder what I taste like.

"Delicious," he murmurs, tugging on my lower lip.

My eyes snap open at his words. Did I say that out loud?

In my surprise, I separate my lips from his, but he's quick to pull my face back down, forcing my lips to meet his once more. When I taste him again, my embarrassment disappears, and I'm once again overwhelmed by my desire for him. His hands travel further up, to my waist and then upper, until he reaches the sides of my bra.

"Can I please take off your shirt?" he whispers against my lips. I nod hastily, pulling away from him briefly so that he can pull the shirt over my head. I'm no longer shy. Why should I be when he probably already saw me like this last night?

The moment the shirt is off, Alessandro's hands land on my hips, holding me up while he takes an eyeful of my body. The way his eyes graze over every inch of my nearly naked body makes me shiver. I'm not even wearing sexy underwear today. *How embarrassing!*

But he doesn't seem to mind, his eyes turning a dark green when they find my breasts. I've never been self-conscious of the size of my breasts, even when all my peers shot right through puberty and had the big chests that strained their school shirts. But now, as I sit in front of Alessandro, and he's staring, I become nervous. He's probably not used to this. He's probably only been with women with big breasts and sexy cleavage. I have neither.

Is it bad that I want to close myself up again now? What if he gets angry again now that my insecurities have popped out and causing me emotional strain again? He won't understand if I tell him the truth, but if I just suddenly close myself off and put the shirt back on, chances are he'll blow up at me and tell me to get out again. I don't even know where I am.

"What's wrong, *amore mio*?" Alessandro asks, brushing a strand of hair out of my face.

He notices things quite quickly. But it's not easy for me to tell him, and he quickly notices that, too.

"Tell me."

"Nothing," I find myself saying with a shrug. He doesn't like this.

"Don't lie to me," he warns. "Tell me what's bothering you."

I sigh, looking down at his chest instead of into his eyes. Staring right into his eyes makes me nervous. I try to distract myself by trailing my fingers across his bare chest, surprised at how hard it is beneath my fingertips.

"*Amore mio*," he calls out, his voice insistent as he grasps my face between his hands and forces me to look at him again. "My love. Talk to me. Please."

The way he hesitates to say the last word tells me he doesn't say it often. Maybe not even at all. I should feel special, but instead, I feel nervous. What if I'm honest with him, and he finds my feelings childish? Like, a woman his age would be confident. I thought I was, too, until I met him. Being with him brings out all my hidden insecurities that I didn't even know existed. Is that a bad thing? Probably.

"How many women have you been with?" I find myself blurting out instead of answering his question. His eyebrows furrow at my question, and a dreadful feeling fills me up when he doesn't answer after a few moments. This is not good. Not at all.

"Does it matter?" he questions. He's dodging the question.

"So . . . that means a lot. Got it," I say with a nod of my

head. I'm trying to act like I'm fine with it, but I'm pretty sure I'm not doing a good job of it, especially when he narrows his eyes at me. I make a move to get off him, but he's quick with his hands, holding me firmly down onto him by my hips.

"Don't be like that," he says.

"Be like what?" I retort.

"Like this. You're becoming cold, closing yourself off from me. I don't like it," he says, a certain unimpressed glint in his eyes.

"Oh, here it is, isn't it?" I snap. "You're going to yell at me again, calling me a child, and then you're going to tell me to get out, aren't you?"

"Don't bring that up like this," he snaps, sitting up with me still on his lap.

"Why not? Why can't I, when it's true?" I exclaim. "My age bothers you, doesn't it? Because not only am I too young, I'm also too childish for you, too, aren't I?"

"It's not like that," he insists.

"You're lying," I say. I know he is. "Why else would you have said all those things to me if it's not?"

He purses his lips, not answering me. I roll my eyes at his silence. Once again, I try to get off him, but he holds me down.

"Let me go," I say.

"No," he firmly says.

"Oh, so now you can talk?" I retort.

"Why are you acting like this?" he snaps.

"Because you're infuriating me," I exclaim, throwing my hands up in the air. "Just be straight with me. Why am I here? Why are you holding me in your arms like this after all that you said to me? Why did you kiss me? Why . . . why did you make me feel wanted?"

The last bit comes out in a whisper, my lips pursing as my gaze falls. Why did I have to add that in the end? I sound so weak, even to my own ears. I bet he didn't sign up for this when he brought me into his bed.

"*Amore mio*," he whispers, his hand touching my cheek and bringing my face up so that we are face-to-face. "I told you the night we met. What did I say to you?"

My eyebrows furrow. What exactly is he referring to, and why can't he just say it himself?

"After you ordered our food at that fast-food restaurant you like so much, what did I tell you?" he clarifies, giving some context to his question. What he said to me after I ordered our food . . . oh! He said . . . he said that he . . . that he . . . "Yes, that. What you are thinking about. It's that. Now say it to me."

"You told me that . . . that you liked me," I mumble.

"*Like, amore mio*," he clarifies, putting emphasis on his first word. "Nothing has changed from that night."

"Even after . . . even after you said all those things to me?" I stutter, choking on a breath.

"Even after all of that. Look, I know that I hurt you, and I regretted it the moment you were gone. I just wasn't man enough to run after you immediately, and that's why you ended up in that situation."

Situation?

"What situation?" I ask, my eyebrows furrowing in confusion.

"*Amore mio*, don't you remember what happened last night? How you got here?" he questions, confusion now visible in his eyes. I shake my head. Now that he's mentioning it, I realise that I never thought about how I ended up here, with him and in his bed. I was too busy trying to get through my embarrassment and be bold with him. And then kissing him.

"What happened last night? The last thing I remember is . . ." Randy. I went to see Randy and took alcohol and cocaine from him. My eyes widen in horror. "Oh no. What did I do?"

He must see the wheels of panic turning in my head because he grabs onto my waist, pulling me against his chest and assures me. "No, don't worry. You didn't do anything bad. If anything, you were taken advantage of."

He mumbles the last part, as if he doesn't want me to hear him, but I do.

"You don't hurt anywhere, right?" he asks, his eyes hesitant. I shake my head in confusion. Why would I be hurting? Just what did happen last night?

"Alessandro, what happened last night? And please don't lie to me," I say, fear slipping into my voice.

"Nothing bad," he rushes out. "You were just really out of it when I arrived, and I could immediately tell that you had drugs in your system."

"What were you doing there?" I ask.

"After finally owning up to what I had done to you, I wanted to make things right, so I had someone track your location, and it led me to that . . . place." The way he says it, that place, he's disgusted.

"You . . . you didn't do anything bad, did you?" I hesitantly ask. The way his eyes darken at my question suggests that maybe he did.

"Nothing . . . *too* bad. I just roughed that guy up a little bit," he admits.

"Randy?"

"Whatever his name is," he grits out. "And don't you dare tell me I was wrong. He fed you drugs when you clearly hadn't taken any before. That bastard was waiting for a chance to take advantage of you."

"And did he? Did he take advantage of me?" I ask, biting my lower lip in fear.

"No," he immediately says. "I got there just in time."

I close my eyes. What was I thinking going there? I get that I was hurt, but going to Randy and using drugs was the worst possible decision I could have made. Oh my . . . what if Alessandro hadn't arrived in time? What if Randy touched me, or worse. What if he raped me? I wouldn't be able to handle it.

"*Amore mio,*" he calls out, stroking my face with his fingers. "It's okay."

"It's not okay," I exclaim, my eyes snapping open. "Things could have gone completely differently. Alessandro, he could have raped me."

Saying the words out loud hurt even more than it did in my head.

"But he didn't," Alessandro persists. "I got there in time, and you're fine. We're all fine."

He says this with such certainty, but the tears won't stop. At this point, I'm sobbing, ugly tears streaming down my face. I must look so unattractive right now. I must look nothing like that night right now. Wait, my face is completely bare. What if he hates it? What if he doesn't like how I look without make-up? These thoughts make the tears worse.

Unable to face him anymore, I lean my head forward, resting the side of my face against his bare shoulder. He doesn't say anything anymore, his arms circling around me and holding me against him as I cry.

How did it get to this? One moment we were kissing, happy, and now I'm crying.

I'm sure he's never had to deal with something like this before. I'm sure none of the previous girls he's had a thing with were such crybabies. I bet they were confident, had no insecurities, and knew how to please him. Before him, I had never touched any man before—I have no experience in this field whatsoever. Finally, we kissed, and then I had to ruin it with my bad thoughts and insecurities. I can't help but think that the further we go into this, the more unsuited I am to him.

He needs someone mature. He needs someone who can give him heirs. He needs someone else. I'm nothing he needs.

"But you're what I want," he murmurs, startling me.

Did I say that out loud?

"Yes, you did."

But just how much did I say out loud? Oh no, does he know of my deepest insecurities now? I don't need him pitying me now, not that I think he's someone to pity another. If anything, he'd laugh and spit in their face.

"Stop it," he reprimands, grabbing my arms and puling me away from him so that he can look into my eyes. "What did I tell you earlier?"

"To stop whatever I was doing in my head," I answer, my lips forming a slight pout.

"And what did you just do?" he questions.

"What you told me not to do," I say.

"Why? What's bothering you so much that you won't even tell me about it?" he questions.

I move to shake my head, but I stop myself. It's no use lying to him anymore. It will only make him angry.

"I . . . it's just . . . I can't." I choke out with a shake of my head.

"Do you need time?" he asks. I merely nod, looking away from him. "Okay."

My head snaps up in surprise. That's all he's going to say? Okay? Is he not going to force me into telling him everything?

"I'm going to give you time, but only if you promise to tell me eventually," he says in warning, and I couldn't have nodded faster.

"I promise," I say.

"Good. Now," he starts, wiping the residue of tears from my eyes and cheeks. "What do you say we get out of bed and get some breakfast? I'm sure you're starving."

"I am," I admit, absentmindedly rubbing my stomach. It's only in this moment that I realise that I'm still only in my underwear and that I have absolutely nothing covering my legs and torso. My cheeks immediately warm up in response to this realisation, and I look down, my eyes finding the shirt on the floor next to the bed.

I bite my lower lip. If I bend down now to pick it up, it'll put my bottom on complete show for him, and I can definitely not trust him not to look.

"Uhm . . . can you perhaps . . . get that that for me?" I timidly ask, pointing to the shirt with my finger. He juts out his lower lip as he appears to think before a wicked glint appears in his eyes.

"I don't know. Can I?" he teases, his hands circling my lower back. "I kind of like you like this. Almost naked, for me only."

He finishes his words off with a bite to my earlobe, and I nearly moan. It takes everything in me not to push him back down and kiss the hell out of him. "No. Give me the shirt."

He playfully raises an eyebrow at me for ordering him around. "No one's ever told me what to do. I usually do that."

"Well, now might be the perfect time for a change," I say, patting his bare chest and trying not to let my eyes wander to his tattoos. If I don't, I might end up exploring all day. "Now get the shirt."

"You're a tease, Havyn Miller," he says, reaching down to grab the shirt.

"How am I being a tease? I'm not even doing anything," I exclaim, staring incredulously at him as he sits up and hands me the shirt.

"Don't act like you don't know the way you look at me," he retorts.

"How do I stare at you?" I question as I slip my arms into the shirt.

"Like you want me to fuck you," he says.

I choke on my spit. Is it really that obvious?

"But it's okay, because I know I stare at you the same way."

He wants me to fuck him? Lord, my thoughts have never been this vulgar before.

"Ahem," I clear my throat. "We should go cook breakfast."

This time, he doesn't stop me from sliding off his lap. I stand completely barefoot on his bedroom floor. "Uhm, could I please get some shoes? And pants, too."

"Shoes I can do. Pants, unfortunately not," he says, lifting the sheets off him. I immediately look away, not wanting to see anything that I shouldn't.

"Why not pants? I'm sure you have many," I say, making sure to keep my eyes off him.

"'Cause I don't want to give them to you," he simply says. My head snaps to his at his words.

"Why not?" I question. Luckily, he's now slipped on a short-sleeve t-shirt and sweatpants so I can look at him comfortably.

"Because I like you only in my shirt," he says, walking over to me with a pair of slippers in his hands.

"Well, I don't, so give me pants," I say, placing my hand on my hip.

"Please, *amore mio*," he scoffs. "I can't find you intimidating when you're so much shorter than I am."

"Well, that's not my fault! It's yours. Why the hell are you so tall in the first place anyway?" I exclaim.

"Stop trying to be tough, my love," he says, and I huff, slipping into the slippers. I squeal when he suddenly lifts me up, and it forces me to wrap my legs around his waist in surprise while his hands hold onto each of my bottom cheeks.

"I'm not trying. I am." I huff, glaring at him.

"Not with me, you're not," he retorts. "With me, you're just a baby."

I hate how he's right. But instead of admitting to it, I merely turn my head away from him.

"What? You hate that I'm right?" he teases.

"Why are you suddenly acting like this?" I exclaim, my head snapping back to his. "You were so mean to everyone at the party."

"Because I like you. I told you that before, too," he says, staring pointedly at me.

I purse my lips, speaking out the words before I can second think it. "How much? How much do you like me?"

Now he purses his lips in thought before finally settling on an answer. "Enough to bring you to my private home where no one besides my best friend and family has ever been."

I'm not sure how much of a big deal that is, but I nod anyway.

"What about you?" he suddenly asks, his question surprising me. "How much do you like me?"

I pretend to purse my lips in thought. I take my own sweet time, but when he starts to impatiently glare at me, I decide to finally answer. "Enough to act like a baby around you."

His lips twitch. He's satisfied with my answer.

And then he starts to carry me out of the room and down the hall to the kitchen. He sets me down on the kitchen island just like yesterday and starts searching through the refrigerator.

"What do you have? I can make us breakfast," I say to him.

He stops and turns to me with narrowed eyes.

"What? After looking after myself for so long, I can cook a meal with almost anything." I shouldn't have just told him that I've been alone for a long time, but he seems to ignore it, turning back to the refrigerator, which I'm grateful for.

"Can you cook?" I decide to ask him. He merely shrugs.

"Does not burning down the kitchen every time I cook count?" he asks, pulling out random food ingredients from the refrigerator.

Not usually, but I'll be nice. "It does," I say.

"What can you make with these?" he asks after setting

everything on the kitchen island beside me. I analyse everything while sifting through recipes in my head.

"How about French toast?" I suggest. Based on what he has, it seems to be the simplest dish I can make.

"Sure," he says with a shrug, as if he doesn't care.

Well, of course. Based on the way he's built, he probably scarfs up all sorts of foods, some of which I may never even have heard of. I jump off the kitchen island and start with the preparations while he gets out his pans and utensils.

When I start using the stove, he stays by me the entire time, alternating between just holding my hand when it's not occupied and full-on hugging me from behind. He's distracting, though, so I say, "You're acting quite clingy, Mr. Mafia."

His chest rumbles from behind me.

"If I didn't know any better, I'd think that you were catching feelings," I tease, waiting for him to deny it. Yes, we have something going on between us right now, but we haven't really labelled it or really talked about it, so I don't expect anything from him.

He doesn't answer.

CHAPTER TWENTY-THREE: HAVYN

I like it in Alessandro's arms.

It's always so warm. *He's* always so warm. It feels like when I'm in his arms and when he's holding me so close to him, nothing else matters. Not who I am, not who he is, and neither of our pasts.

I know deep down that it can't last forever, but while it's here, I want to savour it as much as I can.

"Why are you so quiet, *amore mio*?" Alessandro murmurs into my hair.

"Just thinking," I respond.

"About?" he prods.

"Everything. My life, us," I answer, not bothering to look up at him to see his reaction. Us. Is there even an us? He hasn't mentioned anything, and I don't want to just jump to conclusions on my own. His relationship with Aliya must have just ended recently. Is he ready for another one? With someone ten years his junior?

"Us?" he repeats. I nod. "What about us?"

What are we is what I want to ask, but I keep my mouth sealed shut. What if I ask that, and he responds with something I don't want to hear? Like saying that we're nothing, that we're just having fun. Because this isn't just fun to me. At least I don't think so. But who says he feels the same way? What if he just sees me as a rebound for Aliya, someone to pass the time with before he chooses a wife? The thought hurts. I want to be more to him. I want to *mean* more to him. But right now, that may be too much to ask for.

118

So what now? Should I settle for what we have right now, whatever it is? Just casually kissing and sharing a bed. I'm not sure I can do that.

"Baby," he calls out, grabbing my attention. "Talk to me. Don't shut me out."

He's talking in a gentle tone, but there's an undertone of warning in his voice, and I know why. It's because I've shut him out before, more times than I'd like to admit. But it's not easy to just say what I'm thinking out loud, especially to him, and especially when I'm not certain of how he feels about me.

"It's just . . . there's so much I'm uncertain about," I find myself admitting.

"Such as?" he probes.

"What we are," I hesitate in saying. I close my eyes in panic. I expect him to push me away, to curse at me, but he doesn't. Instead, he grabs my arms and pulls me away from him slightly so that we're face-to-face.

"Look at me," he instructs.

Hesitantly, I open my eyes. I can see in his eyes how vulnerable I look right now.

"What do you think we are?"

I shrug. I don't want to assume. I don't want to get my hopes up. It'll only hurt me in the end.

"What do you want us to be?" he clarifies.

What do I want us to be? A couple. I want us to be a normal couple that goes on regular dates, cuddles, and be silly together. But in his line of work, isn't that too much to ask for? My heart really didn't take all this into account before falling for him.

And then suddenly, something starts ringing, tearing through our moment. His phone. I can't tell whether I'm sad or grateful. He sends me a *sorry* look before lifting me off his lap and getting up. He leaves the room to answer the call. And then my eyes find his wallet that sits on the coffee table. As if in instinct, a certain moment in our date three weeks ago flashes before my eyes, and without even thinking about it, I lean forward, taking his black leather wallet into my hand.

When it comes to opening it, though, I hesitate. What if it's still there? It can't still be there . . . right? Not with me in the picture now at least . . . right?

Pushing my fears away, I open the wallet, and my heart clenches when my eyes land on it. The picture of Aliya. It's still there.

Tears prick at my eyes, and I throw the wallet back onto the coffee table. I want to think that maybe he just forgot to take it out, but that's bull. There's no way you forget to get rid of a picture of your ex-lover when you get a new lover. I knew it. He's not over her. He lied. And I was a fool for believing him.

I need to get out of here.

I get to my feet and rush over to my bag that sits on the kitchen island. I stop to look down at myself. I'm merely in his shirt and slippers, no pants. But if I go back to his room to get pants, he'll stop me and demand that I tell him why I'm suddenly leaving. That'll put me at risk of blurting out all my fears and insecurities. No, I can't do that. He's not worth it.

So I just sling the bag strap over my shoulder and walk to the elevator, and the doors open immediately once I press the golden button. I get onto it, pressing the button for the ground floor. This scene feels so familiar, except this time, Alessandro is not watching me as I leave.

The doors slide close. This is it. If he comes looking for me, I won't let him in. Now I'm certain I'm never coming back here. But then suddenly, I hear a ding, and the doors slide open. My eyes widen when I see Alessandro standing there, his eyes dark.

He doesn't say anything as he stalks into the elevator, causing me to take a step back with every step he takes toward me, and within a few steps, I'm backed up against the elevator wall. He stops right in front of me, placing his hands on either side of my head on the wall, trapping me in.

"Are you jealous?" he taunts me. "Is that why you tried to run from me?"

I don't answer. He doesn't deserve it.

"If you don't answer me, I'll fuck you so hard in this elevator, you won't be able to walk for an entire week," he warns.

There's a promise sealed in his words. He's not bluffing.

I gulp, something suddenly throbbing in between my legs. God dammit, why is this my body's reaction? Why am I so turned on by his words?

Suddenly, I want to take my anger out on him. I want to kiss him senseless and make him feel the rage I feel inside at seeing that picture. But as tempting as angry sex sounds, I won't partake in it, at least not for my first time. But that doesn't mean I can't kiss and touch him.

And so I grab onto him, pulling him down by the collar of his tee and forcing our lips to meet.

Chapter Twenty-four: Havyn

"This doesn't mean anything."

I need to make that clear. I'm just kissing him in order to get rid of all my frustration. It doesn't mean that I'm not still angry at him.

He smiles into the kiss, his hands firmly grabbing my bottom and lifting me up, causing my legs to wrap around his waist. He carries me back into the penthouse, lowering me ever so gently onto the couch before settling on top of me, the most minimal amount of space between the two of us. His tongue invades my mouth like an animal trying to stake its claim. But I can hardly care, not when it feels this good.

Then suddenly, I feel a vibration against my leg. I squirm, wiggling my legs from underneath him. He growls lowly against my lips, his hand coming in between us and then the vibration goes away. I smile against his lips, delving my fingers into his thick tresses of hair. He groans when I tug at the roots.

"Have you ever orgasmed before?" he asks, his voice thick with desire. I can lie and say yes, especially since I don't want him to know that I'm a virgin, but instead, I shake my head in response. A low growl escapes his lips. "The *boys* you've been with before were useless."

I don't miss the way he puts emphasis on the word *boys*.

I can't wait to have my first orgasm, a loud moan escaping my lips as I do.

A few moments of blissful silence go by before I come down from my high, staring up at Alessandro with watery eyes.

"You okay, a*more mio*?" he asks, his voice much gentler than a few moments ago. I nod, and a soft smile graces his lips, his fingers tucking my hair behind my ear. "You look so beautiful, my love. The most beautiful I've ever seen you."

I can't help but blush.

And then the question dawns on me. What now? Yes, he touched me and gave me my first orgasm, but now what? How do I stop things from becoming awkward between us? Wow, this is so stupid. I'm sure he's never had this problem with other women before. And there goes my mind again, going to places it shouldn't be.

And then, as if saved by the bell, the ringing vibration starts again. Alessandro groans, getting off me and leaving the room to answer the phone.

I sit up, running my fingers through my hair.

What in the world did I just do? More importantly, why did I let him do that to me?

Chapter Twenty-five: Alessandro

I'm sporting quite the obvious boner, and it's really uncomfortable.

Lord, when I saw her in that state, I nearly came in my pants. Never has any woman looked more beautiful. That was Havyn in her most raw and vulnerable state. She'd let me do anything to her at that point. If I played my cards right, I know she'd even have let me have fuck her, right there and then.

If only it wasn't for that stupid phone call, which, by the way, was just Eddie checking up on us. It's nice that he cares, but he had terrible timing. I hated to just leave her like that on the couch, so exposed and vulnerable from her first-ever orgasm.

I remember how hesitant she was to tell me she'd never orgasmed before. I proceeded to tell her that the boys she'd been with before were useless. Until . . . I watched her.

My love was a virgin.

That realization did wicked things to me, and that's why I now stand in the shower, fondling myself as I imagine her being in here with me, on her knees, sucking me off.

"Alessandro?" I hear a soft voice call out over the running water. *Amore mio.* I force myself to move faster, chasing my high until I finally come crashing down, releasing everything I have in me. Then I switch off the shower, wrap a towel around my waist, and leave the en-suite bathroom without bothering to dry myself off.

"*Amore mio,*" I call out, watching her turn around to face

me. "Is everything okay?"

"Yeah," she nods, but she looks uncertain. "I just . . . missed you."

My heart warms up in my chest upon hearing her say that. It's only been roughly half an hour since we've seen one another, and she already misses me.

"Oh, I missed you, too, my love," I coo, walking up to her and gathering her in my arms.

"You're wet." she moans, pushing at my chest.

"I don't care," I merely say, placing my one arm under her thighs and picking her up bridal style. She squeals in surprise, instinctively kicking the slippers off her feet in the process. I carry her to my bed where I sit down at the edge and pull her onto my lap. She doesn't say anything, but her face is flushed a deep red.

I can't help but chuckle. We've kissed. We've touched in intimate places. Hell, I even got her off, yet merely sitting on my lap still makes her shy and blush. She's so innocent that it tugs at my heartstrings.

I don't deserve this girl. I know that for a fact. But I can't let any other man have her. I'm a bastard that way.

"Alessandro," she softly calls out.

"Yes, my love?" I hum, placing my lips on her temple.

"Where is this going?" she nervously asks, playing with her fingers. I freeze.

This is a question I was dreading and hoping that, by some miracle, she'd never ask it. But she just did, and now I have to answer her.

The truth is, I can't offer her a normal relationship. Not just because of who I am, but because of the expectations put on me by my father. He still expects me to marry by the end of this month. He even gave me an ultimatum that if I didn't choose a bride before the end of this week, he would choose one for me. It's ridiculous how much power and control my father has when *I'm* the Don, but I can't bring myself to tell him off because, even after everything, he's still my father. The man who raised me. The man who taught me everything I know today. I hate how much I don't want to disappoint him.

A soft sigh pulls me from my thoughts. *Amore mio.*

"Never mind," she says, looking away from me. I want to touch her, to make things right, but I can't. I can't give her false hope. So I stay silent. But honestly, me being silent is more for me than it is for her. I know if she knew I still have to marry soon, she'd never have let me touch her like that. She'd hate me for doing that to her. And despite not being able to give her more, I keep quiet.

I'm a selfish bastard that way.

"You know, I should get going," Havyn suddenly says, and then she's off my lap before I can even react. "I already skipped a day of school. I need to be back tomorrow."

I don't stop her as she gathers her things and disappears into the en-suite bathroom to get changed. A selfish part of me wants to drag her out of there and get her back into my clothes like a fucking caveman, but I resist that part of me.

She deserves better.

Lord, when did I start caring so much about this girl? I don't care about people. That's who I am. That's what I'm famous for. They call me an emotionless monster, and that's okay because that's what I am.

But that was before *her.*

Now, I'm just like any other man who has someone significant in their life. A lover. A partner.

I scoff.

Havyn could never be my partner in life.

Then she emerges from the bathroom, dressed in that skimpy outfit once more. That's not even hers, but I doubt she'd agree to just wear my clothes instead of that. Has her friend even contacted her yet? I doubt it, considering how attentive my love has been to me all day. Some friend.

"Let me walk you out," I say, getting to my feet.

"No," she exclaims, admittedly startling me. "I can go alone. Besides, you're still wet from your shower so . . . it's okay. I'll just go by myself."

The uncomfortableness in her eyes, in her voice, makes me uneasy. I fucked things up just now, but I don't have it in me to fix things. I know exactly what it'd take, but I won't give it to her. I refuse. I have to be a better man than that. At least to her.

Then she's approaching me, stopping right in front of me. She leans up on her tippy toes and places a soft kiss to my jaw. I can't help but smile. She's too short to reach my cheek or lips. Whichever she was aiming for.

"Goodbye, Alessandro."

And that's exactly what that was.

Goodbye.

CHAPTER TWENTY-SIX: HAVYN

Finally, my shift is over.

Adia is waiting for me at one of the tables, busy on her phone, probably with her latest girlfriend. She goes through lovers like underwear, but she seems happy with the way things are, no strings attached, so I find no problem with that.

It's been two weeks since the incident here at the café. Since I kissed Alessandro goodbye. I hadn't meant for it to be a final goodbye, but things just came about that way. After I left his place that day, we just kind of drifted apart. I didn't look for him, and he didn't look for me. I was surprisingly okay with it. Although when he first didn't come for me despite what happened between us, I cried for days. But then I was hit with reality and had to just . . . get over it.

"You done?"

I nod, watching Adia type her last text message before pocketing her phone and getting up. Ever since the incident, I confessed everything to Adia, including my living situation, and I've been living with her ever since. Sure, I go back to her home late and leave before the crack of dawn so that her father doesn't find out, but it's okay. I can't expect too much from her, not when she's dealing with her own stuff.

She's become a lot more comfortable about the lesbian stuff, if I can call it that, but she never goes deep into the encounters she shares with women. I'm thankful for that, though. I'm not really interested in my best friend's sex life.

We take a cab back to Adia's home, and just like every night, I sneak in behind her, being as quiet as possible. I've been doing it for so long now that I've practically become a pro at this. Quite feline.

"God, I'm tired." Adia groans, collapsing onto her bed. I feel the same way. After eight hours of school and then another eight hours at the café, I'm beyond exhausted.

I sit at the edge of the bed.

"You off tomorrow?" Adia asks, crawling towards me on the bed. I nod. Tomorrow is Saturday and my only day off in the week. I usually hide out in Adia's bedroom all day while she brings me food and snacks, and we have a lazy day. "Good, because I need you to come on a date with me."

I blink. What?

"Not like the two of us on a date," she rushes out when I don't respond. "It's just . . . I met this girl, but she's really shy, and she said she'd only meet me if she can bring a friend along. So I agreed, and I kind of told her . . . I'd bring a friend too to go on a double date with us."

"I'm not gay," I say.

"Her friend's a dude. Don't worry. I'd never put you in that situation."

But she'd put me in this one?

"I don't know, Adia," I murmur. "I don't know if I'm ready for a relationship."

"Look, no one said you have to date the guy. It's just one date," she assures me.

I purse my lips. Maybe going on a date would be a good thing. My love life was literally non-existent before Alessandro came into it, and then again after he left it, so maybe this would do me some good. I don't have to go to the date with the mindset of getting a boyfriend, but there's no harm in meeting some new people, people who can actually commit to me.

Before I can even try to talk myself out of it, I nod to Adia, who instantly cheers and pulls me into a tight hug.

She owes me.

I'm glad the date is at a neutral location, so I don't have to dress up too much and won't have to borrow something from Adia's closet. Her clothes are way too revealing for my liking, and this time, I'm going as Havyn. Plain old Havyn Miller. No need to deceive anyone tonight.

As I stare at myself in my denim jumpsuit and faded white sneakers, I feel anxiety start to creep in. What if I'm dressed *too* casually? Yeah, we're going to the café where I work, but I still don't want to underdress.

Shaking off those thoughts, I pull my hair into a high ponytail, and Adia comes out of her closet. Of course, she's dressed to impress, in her bright pink mini-skirt and matching crop top with a pair of heels. Of course she'd wear heels to a date at a *café*.

"You look cute," she comments, smiling at me. Although cute isn't exactly what I was going for, she sounds sincere, so I let it go. It's not like I'm willing to change last minute anyway.

"So tell me about this girl," I say, sitting down on the edge of the bed as Adia starts putting on her jewellery. I don't usually ask about her lovers, but this is the first time she's letting me actually meet one of them. I know it's because she has no other choice, but still.

"Well, her name is Aubrey. She comes from a rich family, just like me, and she's very shy. Like, not yet out the closet shy."

"You're not out of the closet either," I remind her.

"I know," she says with a roll of her eyes. "But at least I'm not scared to be open about my sexuality, with my partners at least. She doesn't even want to be alone with me yet."

"And the guy I'm meeting?" I ask, shifting on purpose.

"Oh, I saw a picture of him. He's cute, and really nice from what Aubrey has said. I think you'll hit it off," she says, although, based on my history, cute and *nice* doesn't seem to be my type. I'll still give it a chance, though. If anything, cute and nice is what I need in my life.

We leave Adia's house and take a cab to the café. It feels weird when I walk in, knowing that I won't be working tonight.

"Over there," Adia says, pulling me to a booth with her. I see the guy first, and he is cute, in an aloof kind of way with his thick-rimmed glasses and his hair that has strands sticking out at random parts of his head. I might be wrong, but he looks kind of familiar. I wonder why . . .

Then I see *her*.

Aubrey. I immediately recognize her.

She was at the party on my date with Alessandro. She was there with her friend, who clearly didn't like me after finding out why I was there. Savannah.

Her eyes widen when she sees me, recognition flashing in her eyes. Clearly, I'm not the same person from that night. How did she not realise that Adia is *the* Adia Hamilton and not me?

"Havyn, you okay?" Adia asks, concern flashing in her eyes.

"Havyn?" Aubrey says out loud in realization. I've been caught out.

"Do you two . . . know each other?" Adia asks, narrowing her eyes at the two of us.

"Of course we do," Aubrey easily says. "We met at a party several weeks ago. She was on a date with my friend's crush."

At first, Adia looks confused until I see the pieces come together in her eyes. They widen, snapping to mine.

"I really didn't think much about when you told me your name, Adia," Aubrey says, standing up. "I thought it was a coincidence at most, especially when I saw your face, but here we are. Care to explain?"

"Its . . . complicated," Adia stammers.

"I have no doubt about that," Aubrey mutters, clearly un-impressed. Why is she taking this so personally, though? We didn't deceive her. It's not like I texted her pretending to be Adia. I feel like the way she's reacting right now is completely unwarranted.

I don't dare say it, though. If I ruin things between Adia and her, Adia will be very angry at me. So, I zip my lip.

"Can we talk in private, please?" Adia requests, staring at Aubrey with desperate eyes. Wow, she must really like Au-brey then.

Aubrey reluctantly nods, and they walk out of the café to have their private conversation.

"So, it's you," my date suddenly says.

"Excuse me?"

"The one who stole Alessandro Romano's heart," he says. My world stills. What?

Then he's standing up, taking off his glasses and shaking his hair, fixing it. Immediately, I know why he seemed famil-iar to me. It's because he is. I've seen him before. At this very café, with Alessandro.

"Nice to meet you, Havyn," he says, holding out his hand for me to take. I don't, though. "I'm Eddie, Alessandro's best friend."

I can't breathe. This is all so much. Too much.

I thought I was catching a break tonight. But boy, was I wrong.

"I-I need to go," I stammer, stumbling back a few steps. Eddie darts forward, grabbing my arm to stop me from fall-ing.

"I'm sorry," he suddenly apologizes. "I didn't mean to spring this on you. I honestly didn't know I was going to be meeting *you* here until I saw you walk in. I really am friends with Aubrey, well, not real friends, I guess, hence the glasses and crappy hairstyle. It's a long story that I won't bother you with."

He's rambling, but I don't have it in me to stop him.

"Why don't you sit down?" he suggests, and despite my brain yelling at me to get out of here, I slump into the seat. Eddie sits opposite me.

"What is it that you want from me?" I ask him.

"Nothing." He shrugs. "I honestly just came here because Aubrey called in a favour. I had no idea I'd run into you here."

"Alessandro . . . he's not anywhere nearby, is he?" I can't help but ask, relief washing over me when Eddie shakes his head.

Then suddenly, Eddie messes up his hair again and puts on the glasses. Adia and Aubrey appear at the table, startling me.

"Everything good?" he asks them, and they nod, exchanging secret smiles. I'm actually happy for them, despite my surprise at Aubrey being gay. Obviously, she doesn't wear it like a flag on her body. She's in the closet for a reason, just like Adia.

"I'm sorry about how I reacted earlier," Aubrey says to me. "I was just . . . shocked, is all."

"It's all good," I tell her. She smiles, grateful.

"Well, since we've cleared the air, how about we ditch this boring café and go somewhere fun?" Aubrey suggests, her eyes lighting up in mischief.

"I like where this is going," Eddie says with a smirk, his eyes only on me. "Lead the way, ladies."

Eddie practically drags me out of the café, silencing all my protests.

Why do I have a bad feeling about this?

CHAPTER TWENTY-SEVEN: HAVYN

A club.
Aubrey brought us to a club.

The moment we get to the entrance, I make a move to turn and walk away, but Eddie's too fast for me, grabbing me and pulling me back. I groan.

"I can't go in here," I tell them. "I'm underaged."

"Not anymore," Adia says with a smirk. What does that mean?

"VIP," Aubrey says to the bouncer, who lets us all in without further questions. I'm immediately overwhelmed by the loud music and flashing neon lights. Suddenly, I'm grateful for Eddie holding me. Otherwise, I'm certain I would get lost all alone in here.

There's so many people, it's like a maze, and I hold onto Eddie tighter, not willing to lose him in the crowd. He understands my action and wraps an arm around my shoulder, holding me against him as he leads me further into the crowd.

Adia and Aubrey steer us up the steel stairs, which immediately lead up to an open-plan area with lush couches and a private bar. And then I notice it. The balloons, the cake. Words on the wall.

Happy Birthday.

"What . . ." I trail off, confused.

Adia turns to me, a smile on her face.

"It's your birthday, silly girl."

It is? I honestly had no idea. It might sound stupid, but with everything that's been going on with school, work, and getting kicked out, I completely forgot about my birthday.

"Guys . . ." I trail off, staring at all the decorations with tears in my eyes.

"No, don't go crying on us now," Adia playfully scolds, pulling me into a hug. "It's your birthday, so no tears."

These are happy tears, though.

"Did you all know about this?" I ask Eddie and Aubrey when I pull away from the hug. They both nod with smiles on their faces. "Wow. This is so . . . nice."

I don't know what else to say. To think, Adia planned all this for me with the help of two strangers who don't even know me. It's just . . . so nice.

"Now, since you are legal now, Ms. Eighteen-year-old— let's get you a drink," Aubrey says. Her mood and attitude towards me has completely changed since earlier when she found out who I am. Now she's treating me like we're actually friends, and I can't help but think. Maybe, just maybe, we really can be friends. Especially if this lasts between her and Adia.

"What can I get you?" the bartender asks when we get to the bar.

"Let's get her started with a Sex on the Beach," Aubrey says before I can even think of what I want.

"You'll thank me later," she says, flashing me a wink. "So, how are you looking to spend the last of your birthday night? You wanna get completely hammered, or do you want to get laid?"

"Neither of that," I say. I'm not about to get piss drunk here, and I'm definitely not losing my virginity to a complete stranger tonight. No thank you.

She nods thoughtfully.

"Then let's just party. We have delicious cake, too," she suggests, and I nod.

I go to sit on the couch next to Eddie instead of Adia, who

I expect is keeping the space next to her empty for Aubrey. Aubrey brings my drink soon and insists that I try it. The moment the drink touches my tongue, a burst of flavour erupts in my mouth. It's really fruity, with a certain tartness that doesn't allow the sweetness to be overwhelming.

The three of them stare at me expectantly. And then I break out into a smile.

"I like it."

They cheer before Eddie gets to cutting the cake. It's a plain vanilla cake with butter icing on top, just how I like it. We each get a slice, and I moan in delight. The cake and the cocktail together are surprisingly really good.

One drink turns into two, and two turns into five, and before I even realise it myself, I'm drunk.

I giggle, leaning into Eddie's side.

"Oh, I know someone who won't be pleased to see that," Aubrey says, pointing at us.

"Should I call him?" Eddie asks, and she shrugs, leaning into Adia.

"Who are you calling?" I ask Eddie when he takes out his phone and starts dialling a number.

"Someone who's missed you quite a lot," Eddie says before pressing *call*. I close my eyes, leaning my head on his shoulder as he talks into the phone. Too bad the music is too loud for me to hear.

"I'm getting another drink," I suddenly announce, startling them. Before any of them can stop me, I prance over to the bar, flashing the bartender a flirtatious smile. God, where did all this confidence come from?

"The usual?" he asks, and I nod. God, I've had so many, it's become my usual now. He whips up my drink quickly and hands the colourful alcohol in a glass to me. I tip it back, gulping the whole drink down in one go.

I smile when it's all up, slamming the glass onto the bar

counter. Then I go back to the couch, this time, jumping onto Eddie's lap. He freezes under me, his eyes widening.

"Eddie, you're so warm, you know that?" I murmur, resting the side of my face on his shoulder. "And so comfortable."

"Why? Because I won't hit on you?" he retorts, and I find myself nodding. It's true, though. I can be on his lap, and he won't hit on me, hence this situation right now. I guess it's because Alessandro is his best friend. He must know our history.

Alessandro . . .

I choke up a sob.

"Hey, what's wrong?" Eddie asks, concern in his voice. I sniffle, looking up at him.

"What's wrong with your friend?" I cry out. "Why didn't he come for me?"

Eddie's eyes widen.

"Why did he leave me?" I cry out. "Didn't he like me?"

"I honestly don't know," he admits, rubbing my back. "I'm sorry, little girl."

I sniffle, pulling up my nose.

"I hate him," I exclaim. "I hate him for making me feel cared for and then just abandoning me."

Eddie sighs but doesn't say anything. More like he doesn't know what to say to me.

And then I hear it.

"*Amore mio.*"

Chapter Twenty-eight: Havyn

I must be dreaming.

There's no way I just heard that. There's no way I just heard *him*.

"*Amore mio.*"

There it is again. I scoff. I must be losing my mind.

There's no way he's here. He wouldn't dare come here after everything. After all this time.

Then suddenly, I'm pulled off Eddie's lap and into another person's arms. I fight against their hold, thrashing my arms and legs.

"My love," the voice calls out again, and I freeze. "It's me."

I look up, my eyes widening when they meet *his*.

Alessandro.

And then the sniffles start again.

"You're here?" I sniffle, and he nods. "Why? Why are you here?"

I punch my little fists into his chest, but I don't think he even feels it. He's too strong, and I'm too weak.

"How dare you . . . come here . . ." I trail off, my punches ceasing. Now I'm full-on crying, burying my face in his shoulder.

"I'm sorry, my love," he says to me, his hold on me tightening. "I'm really sorry."

"It's too late," I mumble, my eyes fluttering closed. "It's too late . . ."

And then I'm out like a light.

When I wake up, I'm in Alessandro's car. We're on the highway, driving to who knows where. I notice the jacket thrown over me. He must have put it there.

I lean my head against the window, closing my eyes again.

When I open my eyes again, I'm back in Alessandro's arms. Then I hear the sound of an elevator dinging. I pop open a single eye to scan my surroundings.

My other eye instinctively opens. I'm at his place. He brought me home with him.

I should fight him. I should protest. I should demand he take me back. But I don't. Instead, I just lean further into him.

I missed this. Being touched by him. Being in his arms.

It feels like after a long time, I've finally come home. And that's dangerous. I know that better than anyone.

He carries me straight to his bedroom, placing me gently onto his bed. I want to just lie there, hoping that he'll join me and hold me in his arms through the night, but my body has other plans.

Because just at that moment, everything I ingested comes right up, and I'm bending over, emptying my stomach onto the floor, onto his precious carpet. He's by my side in a single moment, rubbing my back.

"I'm sorry," I mumble, feeling acid build up in my chest once more.

"It's okay," he assures me, both his voice and his touch soothing. "Let it all out."

And I do, puking until I have nothing left in me.

Now all I can do is stare down at the mess I made. I can't believe it. I vomited in front of Alessandro, all over the carpet in his bedroom. How embarrassing.

He doesn't seem to be bothered by this, though, gathering me back in his arms and carrying me into the en-suite bathroom. He places me on the toilet seat and grabs a face towel from the rack along with a cup of water. He brings the cup to my lips, and I let the water in, gargling for as long as I can to erase any and all traces of the vomit from my mouth before spitting it back into the cup. He then proceeds to wipe the sides of my mouth with the towel. I just sit still and silent as he cleans up where I messed on my face.

He's being so caring right now. He's actually taking care of me right now.

As much as I want this to last forever, I want him to stop. He's giving me false hope. That maybe he actually cares about me. That maybe I actually mean something to him.

He takes a step back and starts running the bath. I watch him as the water fills the tub. He's wearing a single pair of dark grey sweats with a loose black shirt on top. It's short-sleeved, leaving his tattooed arms fully on display.

When the tub is full, he drops in some bath salts and then comes back to me, pulling me up. When his hand starts pulling the strap of my jumpsuit down my shoulder, I freeze. He notices, and his movements stop.

"Can you undress yourself?" he asks me, his voice throaty.

Considering the fact that I'm only staying upright because he's holding on to me, I'm gonna say *no,* so I shake my head.

"Then let me. I won't do anything else. I promise."

I nod, letting him pull the jumpsuit down my body until it lies in a puddle at my feet. He lifts up one foot at a time to get me out of the jumpsuit completely before standing back up. I lift my arms up in the air, letting him pull the t-shirt I was wearing underneath over my head. He tosses it aside, now leaving me in just a bra and panties. They're not even matching. *Lord.*

How unattractive.

"I'm going to take off your underwear now," he tells me, and I nod, gulping.

I realise this is going to be the first time he's going to see me completely naked. If I was sober, I'd definitely attempt to cover myself, but in my drunken state, I can't bother, not even when he tosses my undergarments aside.

He picks me up again and gently places me in the tub.

I sigh in delight when my body is surrounded by nice warm water and bubbles. I lean my head against the bath, closing my eyes. Alessandro walks out to clean up the mess I made inside, and if I wasn't so out of it right now, I'd offer to do it myself. I feel bad, but this bath feels so good.

The bathroom door opens again, and I know that Alessandro has walked in. I can smell him.

Then I feel his hand on my face, caressing my skin gently. Tenderly.

"I'm so sorry, *amore mio*," he whispers. "I wish I could make it all up to you."

I want you to, my heart whispers in my chest.

I want *you*.

Still. After everything. I still want him. I want all of him. For myself. To be mine.

I've never felt this way before. This possessiveness over something, but with him, it comes to me naturally. I don't care if I sound like a caveman. I want him to be *mine*, just as much as I've always been his.

From the moment we met, from the moment he saved me, he had my heart. And now, I want his, too.

"Get in here with me," I murmur, my eyes fluttering open. "Please."

He doesn't hesitate to strip out of his clothes until he's standing completely naked in front of me, in all his beauty and glory. This is the first time I'm seeing him naked, too, and he's everything I imagined him to be and more.

His body is a piece of art, almost every inch inked, and his . . .

I look down, my face warming up.

Then his finger is under my chin, tilting my head up so that I'm looking at him again. He doesn't say a word, but I know. So I look at him again, properly this time without hesitating.

He's so big and stands up straight against his abs.

I've never seen one before, but even I know that his package is impressive. Then, when I'm done, I look away, scooting forward in the tub. He slips in behind me, opening his legs so that I can sit in between them.

He presses himself against my back, and I gasp. He's so . . . hard.

He wraps his arms around my front, pulling me back until I'm resting my back against his chest. My eyes flutter closed again, and I release a satisfied breath. This is it. I never want this moment to end. His lips are at my temple, brushing ever so gently against my skin.

I hum, snuggling into him in the water. He becomes harder with every movement I make, and although I fear I may be hurting him, I don't stop. Because he doesn't stop me either.

Then I twist my body around in his hold to face him. His eyes are closed, his eyebrows pinched together. Almost as if he's holding himself back. Maybe he is.

"Alessandro," I murmur, cupping his face in my soapy hands. His eyes flutter open, and I give him a small smile, unable to stop myself.

"Why are you looking at me like that?" he asks. I smile wider.

"Because I like you."

There is it. I said it. I said those words that I've never uttered to him before.

He freezes, clearly not having expected me to suddenly confess to him. But it had to be done. I had to get it off my chest.

Then I wrap one of my hands around him, and a moan escapes his lips. I silence it with a kiss, delving my free hand into his hair. He responds immediately, his fingers gripping my bare skin, as if I'll disappear if he lets go.

I'm not going anywhere, though.

He's so big that my hand can't even wrap around him completely. I start stroking him, moving my hand up and down his thick length. I'm not even sure if I'm doing it right, whatever *it* is.

A hand job?

But his silent little moans into my mouth spurs me on to move my hand faster. I must be doing something right then.

And then he's coming, spurting all over my hand. It washes away with the water, but not before I feel it. It's thick, hot, and sticky. A texture I've never felt before.

Now that I've touched him, I can't help but wonder. What does he taste like?

"Baby," he says, breathing out, breaking the kiss. "You're absolutely amazing."

I grin, placing a soft kiss on his lips. I'll never forget his moans and the sounds he makes when he comes. It's a guttural sound coming from deep within his throat. It makes me feel good.

He kisses me again, his tongue delving into my mouth. He wraps his arms around me, pulling me forward until my body is pressed right against his. He hardens underneath me again, and I moan. I'm doing that to him. Not some other girl. But me. Havyn Miller.

And there's no better feeling.

Chapter Twenty-nine: Alessandro

"What did you just say?"

My father and both my brothers blink at me in shock—in disbelief. They're certainly hoping they heard me wrong, but they didn't.

"I said, I'm not marrying the woman you've chosen for me," I say, quite firmly to make sure they know I'm being serious. Ironically, my father chose Adia Hamilton to be my bride because I was taking too long to make a decision, but I just refused. I can't marry her. I won't.

Not only is she not even into men, but I also have feelings for her friend. Her friend whom I refuse to hurt any further.

"And why not?" Father questions, his eye twitching at my defiance. He's shocked, of course, because throughout my entire life, I've never gone against him. I've never said no to him. This is the first time.

"I'm just not ready to get married yet," I lie. Father slams his fist onto the table. He's fuming. But before he can tell me off, I'm standing up. "Goodbye then."

Then I'm walking out.

My youngest brother, Luciano, follows after me, all the way out of our family home.

"Brother," he calls out, and I come to a stop, only because it's him. I wouldn't do the same for our eldest brother, Dante.

"If you're here to try and convince me to marry that woman, it won't work," I say to him, but he shakes his head.

"I'm not here to try and talk you into doing anything you don't want to do," he assures me. "I just . . . have one question."

"And what's that?"

"Who is she?" he asks, his lips forming a grin.

I chuckle, shaking my head. He may be five years younger than me, but he sees right through me. Back there, I tried to play it off like I just didn't want to get married, but Luciano saw right through that. He knows there's a girl involved. "There *is* a girl, isn't there?"

He sounds almost disappointed at the fact that there might not even be a girl involved here. I know why. If there's one person who's been praying for love to come into my life, it's Luciano. He always told me that one day, someone would appear and break down the walls I've built around my heart. He's been waiting for this day for so long.

"There is someone," I say in confirmation, and he silently cheers as to not get anyone's attention.

"Who is she? What's her name? What family is she from?" He bombards me with questions.

"Well, I can't tell you too much about her yet, but her name is Havyn, and she's a commoner," I tell him.

"A commoner?" he repeats, and I nod. Then he smiles. "I always knew it wouldn't be one of those rich bitches who would steal your heart. They're too fake."

Says the guy with the biggest crush on a girl who comes from one of the wealthiest families in Italy. I don't bring her up, though. I know better than to do that.

"Anyway, I'm happy for you," he tells me, and I can tell that he's being sincere. "I really hope things work out for the two of you."

Me, too.

I wait for Havyn outside her school.

She doesn't know that I'm coming to pick her up today. It's a surprise, one I know she'll love.

The school bell rings, and students immediately start

filtering out through the school doors. I get out of my car and come to stand against it. I want Havyn to be able to see me.

The moment I'm in sight, though, everyone stops walking and talking and just stares at me with wide eyes and slacked jaws. Of course. They're all probably wondering what I'm doing here. I've got no business here. Although, that was the past. Now, I have business here. Especially when someone very special to me attends here.

A group of three girls are brave enough to approach me, two of them looking absolutely terrified while the one in the middle holds her head up high, radiating faux confidence that I know I can knock down in a single moment.

"Mr Romano," she greets. At least she has enough manners to not call me by my first name. I hate strangers calling me by my first name with a sense of familiarity. It pisses me off. "What brings you to *my* school?"

My school? Is her father the principal here or something?

"How is that any of your business?" I snap. I honestly don't have time for girls like her. I'm just here for *my* girl, and then I'm leaving this dump called a school. If it weren't her senior year, I'd have her transfer to another school, a private school where I know she won't be messed with.

The girl flinches but manages to compose herself again quite quickly. I'll admit, it's impressive.

"I was just curious," she says. "I'm very curious, you see. About you."

The way she bats her eyelashes at me, biting her lip seductively, does nothing to me. This girl can't make me hard. Not even close.

"Well, you should stop being curious about me," I say, standing upright from leaning against the car. "I'm not someone *anyone* can simply be curious about."

Something flashes in her eyes. Something like embarrassment. Good. She's no one in this world, and she needs to know that.

Then my eyes land on something metres behind her. Or rather, someone.

Amore mio.

She's staring right back at me, her eyes wide and a smile on her face. I smile back, but then her eyes move to the girls in front of me, and just like that, the pleasant smile is gone. It's replaced by something darker, and she clenches her hands into fists at her sides.

My love is jealous.

It makes me twitch in my pants. Now that's what gets me hard. *She's* what gets me hard.

She stomps over to us, the girls in front of me finally taking notice of her only when she's standing right behind them and my eyes are clearly on her.

"Can I help you?"

"Move," my love spits out, her voice dripping with venom. I can't help but smile. I'm no stranger to women getting jealous over me, but this is something different. She's so young, yet she's filled with so much fire in her, it's so fucking sexy.

If we weren't in public right now and I knew she wouldn't mind, I'd have her against my car already with my hand up her skirt to feel *just* how jealous she is. I bet this all makes her wet. The thought just makes me harder, to the point that I ache to be released from my cotton binds.

"Who are you?" the girl in the middle snaps at my love, who doesn't take a single word further before she pushes her out of the way. Then, to my shock, she launches herself at me, pressing her mouth to mine.

I freeze, my eyes wide.

Havyn has never been one for public displays of affection, she's made that very clear to me. But here she is, kissing me in front of the entire school, and I'm not a normal man that she's kissing.

I'm the Don.

It doesn't take me long to snap out of it, though, and my body moves on its own, my hands gripping her hips as I tilt my head to deepen the kiss. She moans into my mouth, and, as if she just realised what she's done, she starts to pull away, but I follow her with my lips, not letting her break the kiss.

I cup her firm bottom in my hands, pulling her flush against me, and she gasps when she feels just how hard I am for her. The thought has me almost lifting her skirt and touching her to see if she is indeed wet. Almost, though. The thought of horny teenage boys getting a flash of her underwear puts me off.

But I still need her. I need her so badly it's literally painful.

And so I force myself to break the kiss. She looks utterly fucked when I do. Her lips are swollen, her cheeks flushed, and the lust is evident in her eyes. I bet I look the same.

Without another glance at the girl still standing by us, completely stunned, I let Havyn into my car before getting in myself and driving off.

The car ride is silent. The only sounds I can hear are the heaving of Havyn's chest, rising up and down. Up and down.

I reach over the console and place my hand on her bare thigh. She tenses under my touch but doesn't push my hand away. She just lets it rest there, staring down at it with big eyes. I squeeze her flesh before pulling away, ignoring the disappointed look on my love's face.

I can't touch her right now. If I do, I'm afraid I won't be able to control myself. If I do, I'll end up pulling over on the side of the road and fucking her in this very car, and as tempting as that sounds, I don't want our first time to be in my car. I don't want *her* first time to be in my car.

So I restrain myself. Because I know she deserves better. She deserves to be wooed, and prepped with at least two orgasms so that she's nice and slick to take me inside her. She deserves a bed, and candles with mood lighting. All that shit. Not just a quick fuck. And although I'm inexperienced in that area, I'll do my best. For *her*.

I glance at her for a quick moment. Is she ready? For me? For all that I have to offer? For all the baggage I come with? She seems keen to be with me in general, but does she understand the implications that come with being with me? I don't think she's actually thought it through. As much as I want her to keep being delusional with her head in the clouds, I can't do that to her. I *won't* do that to her.

So I think it's time that we sit down and talk about this.

I pull up to my apartment building, leading Havyn all the way to my penthouse with a soft touch to her lower back. Surprisingly, she doesn't ask why we're here. It's almost like she doesn't even care. Like she trusts me *that* much.

I lead her to the couch, pulling her down to sit next to me. It's only now that her eyebrows furrow.

"Is something the matter?" she softly asks, concern evident in her voice.

"We . . . need to talk," I say, cringing at how that sounds. Her face falls, reminding me of just how bad my choice of words sounded.

"Did I do something wrong?" she asks.

I shake my head, grabbing her hand. "You didn't do anything wrong, my love," I assure her.

"Then?"

"You asked me a question before, and I didn't answer you," I say, and recognition flashes in her eyes. She knows what I'm referring to. Good. "The truth is, I knew back then where things were going between us, and that's why I pulled back. And it's not because I don't want a relationship with you. It's because I know I can't be what you need me to be."

"I don't understand," she says.

"*Amore mio*, I'm not an ordinary man. I don't have an

ordinary job. I don't come from an ordinary family. I'm not a good man." I start off by giving her a stern look when she opens her mouth to protest. She needs to hear everything I have to say first before she protests, because I know this can change everything, including how she feels about me. "I've done many wrong things, terrible things, in my lifetime. I've killed more people than I'm willing to admit to you, and as much as it will repulse you, I *enjoyed* it. I enjoyed having that power over someone's life, and then taking it away just as they plead for mercy. But that's not all. My father will also never accept you. You don't come from a rich, well-known family, and you don't have any ties to our world. If we end up doing this, you'll have to be prepared to never be accepted by my family, never be respected as a new member of my family, as my *wife*."

Yes. I said it. Wife.

I've made a decision. Even after all of this, if she still wants me, I'm going to make her my wife. No questions asked.

"You'll also be in danger as my partner as I have many enemies, but if you decide to be with me still, I'll protect you with my life. I can promise you that."

She just stares at me.

"Anyway, if you decide you don't—"

She cuts me off with a kiss. She pulls away before I can even comprehend what's happening, cupping my face in her hands.

"Of course I still want this," she says, breathing out, like she's on the verge of tears. "I didn't go into this blind, Alessandro. I knew exactly who you were from the beginning, and I still fell for you. All of this . . . what you're telling me, none of it scares me. I'm prepared for all of it. As long as I can be with you."

I kiss her, tasting her salty tears on my tongue.

God. I think I might love her.

CHAPTER THIRTY: HAVYN

"And this is my brother, Luciano."

I smile as I stare at the pictures Alessandro is showing me. So far, he's shown me a picture of his father, who's, and I quote, *someone to look out for*, his mother, and then he shows me a picture of his younger brother, Luciano. He's a real cutie, and that's saying a lot since he's all man, but there's something different to him, with that messy hair identical to his brother's, yet those mischievous eyes and cheeky smile. I never thought I'd see a man from a mafia family smile so broadly.

"But didn't you say you have two brothers? Where's the other one?" I ask, staring up at him. We're lying in bed, and he sits back against the headboard with me next to him, leaning my head on his broad shoulder.

"We don't really talk about him. He's . . . he's not a good man," he admits. "He also hates me for becoming Don when it's all he's wanted his entire life."

I don't want to say I understand, but if something you've been yearning to have all your life suddenly gets taken away . . .

"He's the oldest, so he was supposed to be Don. But even father didn't deem him fit for the position," Alessandro says.

"Why?" I can't help but ask.

"He's problematic. Reckless. Cruel. He doesn't care about anyone but himself. If he had the chance, he'd ruin the empire just for the sake of it. Father couldn't trust him with the empire, so he chose me to become Don."

"Then it's understandable that he didn't get chosen," I say. He nods.

"I have to admit, though . . . I do feel sorry for him at times," Alessandro admits, appearing to cringe at the very admission. "He has a different mother from Luciano and I, making him only our half-brother. My father was very cruel to him, ever since he was young. There was so much expectation put on him. I can imagine how he must have felt, as a mere ten-year-old boy, forced to commit your first murder."

I wince. That is cruel.

"He spent his entire life training to take over the empire. He never did anything to disappoint anyone. He was basically the perfect son, the perfect heir."

"Then what happened?" I ask.

"I'm not sure, to be honest. Just one day, he suddenly changed. He became reckless. Started killing people left, right, and centre with no care for who our allies are. He ruined so many alliances we had with foreign mafias when he went on his killing spree. But . . . I have a suspicion. I'm not sure if I'm right, but I think that I am."

"What is it?"

"I think there was a woman," he says, his eyes meeting mine. "I think my brother was in love. And she betrayed him."

I can't stop thinking about what Alessandro told me.

His brother was in love . . . and he got betrayed? By the very woman he loved? By the person who was supposed to love him back? Care for him. Protect him.

Dante definitely turned out the wrong way in the end, but even I feel sorry for him.

I look at Alessandro, who's cooking us dinner. What would I do if he betrayed me? What would he do if *I* betrayed him?

I shake off the thought. I'd never do that to him, and I know he'd never do that to me. Not after everything we've been through to finally be together.

"What are you thinking about, my love?" Alessandro asks, stepping away from the pot and between my legs as I sit on the kitchen island. It's my favourite place to be when he's in the kitchen, right here by him.

"Just . . . us," I admit.

"Us?"

I nod.

"How far we've come," I say, placing my hands on his shoulders. He looks so husband-ey and domestic, with the apron that I made him wear and the spoon in his hand. "I'd like to think we're not still the people we were when we first met."

"We're not," he insists. "I was a cold-hearted bastard back then. With no feelings. *You* awakened feelings in me that night, feelings I never thought were possible for me to feel. It was fate for us to meet. You changed me for the better."

"You changed me, too," I tell him, and it's true. "After losing everyone I loved, my family, my mom . . . I was a shell of my former self. I didn't find happiness in anything, or anyone. I just lived my life on autopilot, waiting for the day that I finally leave this place. But you . . . you changed that. You showed me that I could be happy again. With you. You, too, taught me how to feel, and I'll always be grateful to you for that."

His eyes glisten with unspoken emotions.

Then he drops the spoon and envelops me in his arms, his lips coming down on mine. I moan, wrapping my arms around his neck.

I'll never get tired of kissing him. Him, his taste, is like a drug, and I'm more than willing to be high on him 24-7. The way he's kissing me, it's fierce, fiercer than any other kiss before, and suddenly, I know where this is going. And I want it to go there. I want to go all the way. With him.

Pressing my pelvis against his, I gasp to find him rock hard in his pants.

"*Amore mio*," he says, breaking away from me. "If we don't stop now —"

"I don't want to stop," I say, cutting him off. "I want this. I want *you*."

He growls, grabbing a fistful of my hair and kissing me again. He's rough with this kiss, almost feral, as if he can't get enough of it. Of me.

Then I remember.

"Alessandro, the food —"

"It's done." He dismisses my worries, pulling the apron off his body. I can't help but giggle. He's in such a hurry, so impatient, like he's been waiting a long time for this. I know I have.

He then grabs me, and I wrap my legs around his waist, letting him carry me to the bedroom. When he lays me on the bed and crawls over me, everything suddenly becomes real. This is really happening. I'm going to have sex with this man. I'm going to lose my virginity. And I'm ready. I want it. I want it all with *him*.

When he kisses me, all my nerves wash away. I bury my fingers in his thick tresses, tugging at the roots until he moans into my mouth. He pulls away to unbutton his shirt that I'm wearing. He does it slowly, undoing one button at a time. I close my eyes, knowing exactly what he's going to see when it's off.

I'm not sure why, but this morning, I made a decision. I put on the one set of lingerie that I own. It's nothing special, just a matching pair of lacy red bra and panties, although it's completely see-through, meaning that he can see my mound and my nipples completely. When the shirt is off me, he sucks in a breath. I open my eyes, desire washing over me when I see the way he's looking at me.

He looks so hungry, his pupils are dilated, and his eye-lashes are fluttering.

"Do . . . do you like it?" I hesitantly ask. His eyes snap up to mine.

"Like it?" he repeats, scoffing in disbelief. "I fucking love it."

Then his mouth latches onto my left nipple, right over the lacy fabric. I moan, arching my back off the bed.

"So. Fucking. Sexy," he praises, swirling his tongue around me. If it feels this good with his mouth over the fabric, I can't even imagine what it will feel like when there's nothing separating me from his mouth, from his tongue.

His hand travels down, cupping me down there. I gasp.

"So fucking wet," he says, rubbing me through my panties. I can feel exactly how wet I am. My panties are damp to the point that my arousal leaks through, coating his fingers. I should feel embarrassed by how turned on I am by mess on his fingers, but I'm not. I'm more aroused than ever.

Moan after moan tumbles from my lips as he continuously flicks his tongue on my nipple, and his hand rubs against me, and before I even realise it, I come crashing down with the loudest moan yet. My body collapses against the bed, sweat coating my temples.

Alessandro pulls away to look at me, a satisfied smirk on his face.

"Do you think you can come for me again?" he asks, his fingers touching my sensitive skin once more.

"Are we not going to—"

"Patience," he murmurs. "Patience, *amore mio.*"

His pet name for me has never sounded dirtier.

"Look down, my love," he says, rubbing me through my soaked panties. "Look at yourself."

I do, my cheeks flushing with heat when I do. His fingers

are soaked in my arousal, but he doesn't stop touching me, rubbing me.

"Is this all for me?" he asks, and I immediately nod.

"All for you," I promise.

Then he's tearing my panties, the fabric shredding before he tosses it aside. He crawls down my body, laying kisses all over my skin as he does, until his head is in between my legs, his breath fanning me. I close my eyes. He's face-to-face with my most sensitive part, and it's making me even wetter.

"Look at me, a*more mio*," he commands, and my eyes snap open. I look down once again.

Then suddenly his mouth latches onto my clit, and he starts sucking. I gasp at the foreign sensation. It's certainly different, something I've never experienced before, but it feels . . . wow. I can't even describe it in words. It feels *that* good.

Then his lips travel down, and he thrusts his tongue inside me. I moan out loud, arching my back. His tongue moves in and out of me with a rhythm. He alternates between thrusting, licking, and sucking, and all too soon, I feel that rush returning, and I know I'm about to come again. Alessandro seems to realise this because he moves his tongue faster, his fingers reaching up to pinch my clit, and with that final suck, I come all over his face.

"Ah!" I moan, embarrassment creeping in when I realise that I just squirted all over his face and mouth. He sits up, licking my arousal off his lips. Then he kisses me, moaning as I taste myself on his tongue.

"Now," he says, breaking the kiss. "Let's take this off."

He tugs my bra strap, and I lift my back, letting him unclip the clasp before pulling the bra off my shoulders and tossing it aside. He then strips out of his pants and shirt, his erection standing proudly against his abs. I stare at it with big eyes. Even though I've seen him once before, he's still very impressive, and very *big*.

"Condom?" he huskily asks, but I shake my head. "Good."

I want to feel him bare, even if it's just for the first time. I'm not on birth control, so this might be reckless, but I want to feel *him* with nothing separating us.

He positions himself between my legs, rubbing himself against my wet folds. I suck in a deep breath, preparing myself for the intrusion.

"Breathe, baby," he coaxes, his voice soft.

"Won't it hurt?"

"It'll hurt at first, but I'll make it good for you. I promise."

I nod, releasing the breath I held in. Then he nudges himself at my entrance, my body involuntarily tensing up.

"Relax," he says, soothing my tension with a kiss to my face.

I nod, staring into his eyes.

"I'll take it slow."

Then he starts pushing inside, and I wince, taking him in inch by inch. It burns, but it's not *that* bad. I can handle this much pain. Then it hurts, and I can't take it anymore, so I wrap my legs around him, digging the heels of my feet into his back, pushing the rest of him inside me with one single movement.

We gasp in unison when he's fully inside me.

"It's okay. It's okay, my love," he says, soothing me and placing kisses all over my face.

I squirm under him, and he grabs my hips, stopping me.

"Stop moving," he commands, and I do.

"You can move," I tell him once the pain subsides a little.

"I will. Just give me a moment," he groans. "You're so fucking tight. If I move too fast, I'll combust, and that will be very embarrassing for me."

I shake my head. I want him to lose control. I want him to lose himself inside me.

So I clench around him, and he groans.

"Fuck, you're killing me, baby."

I can't help but smile. I love the effect I have on him.

Then he starts pulling out until only the tip is inside me, before pushing back in with a single thrust. I moan, the pain completely gone. Now, all that remains is the pleasure. He moves in and out of me in a rhythm, and I grip his shoulders, spreading my legs further to let him in. This allows him to enter me at a deeper angle, and he moans, his length hitting a spot inside me that has me seeing stars.

"Faster," I plead. "Please."

He listens, pounding into me, faster and faster with each thrust. I can hardly take all the pleasure anymore, already overstimulated from my previous two orgasms.

"That's right. Take me. Take all of me," he praises, rocking in and out of me.

Then he reaches down and pinches my clit, causing me to gasp and abruptly come for the third time in a row. He continues moving in and out of me, chasing his own orgasm, and with one final thrust, he erupts inside me, filling me to the brim. He continues rocking in and out of me slowly, riding out his orgasm. When he pulls out, I feel so empty yet so full of all his cum.

He collapses next to me, pulling me into his arms. Our sweaty bodies stick together, but we couldn't care less.

"That was . . ."

"Amazing," I finish for him.

"Completely and utterly amazing." He breathes out, rolling onto his side so that we are lying face-to-face. "You're amazing, you know that?"

I blush.

I'm really glad it was as good for him as it was for me, especially considering that it was my first time, and I had no prior experience on what to do.

"You're absolutely perfect," he whispers. "For me. Just for

me."

"And so are you," I tell him, and it's true.

He's everything I've ever wanted and more.

And I'm never letting him go.

CHAPTER THIRTY-ONE: HAVYN

The next few days pass by in a blur.

Alessandro and I spend most of the time ravaging one another and only leaving the bed to eat. He even took a break from his work, leaving his best friend, Eddie, in charge in the meantime. But now, today, he has to return to work.

I pout, lying naked under the covers, watching as he gets dressed.

"Don't look at me like that, my love," he says, staring pointedly at me. "You're making me feel guilty."

"That was the point," I shamelessly say.

He shakes his head with a chuckle. "I'll try to be back as early as I can, okay?" he says, rounding the bed to come stand by my side, fully dressed, to my dismay. I nod, puckering my lips up to him. He chuckles, leaning down and placing a soft kiss to my lips. He pulls away before I can deepen the kiss, already knowing what I was about to try to do. He knows if I continue, he'll end up never leaving.

When Alessandro's gone, I get dressed, and by that, I mean I just put on one of his shirts. I've gotten used to walking around here in just his shirt with nothing underneath. In fact, I think he'll quite like coming home to me like this.

Then suddenly, the elevator dings. Furrowing my eyebrows in confusion, I leave the room and walk to the living room. The elevator doors are closed, and it dings again. Looks like someone wants to come inside.

"Alessandro," I call out, walking to the elevator. I press the button to open the elevator doors. "Are you trying to trick me — "

I cut myself off when I come face-to-face with a gun. I freeze, my eyes widening. In front of me stands a man dressed completely in black with a black peak cap on and a balaclava covering his face, and he's holding a gun out, aiming right at my own face.

"What . . . what do you want?" I stammer, holding my hands up in the air.

"Havyn Miller?" he asks instead of answering my question. I nod, gulping.

He steps forward, and then unexpectedly, he grabs me, pulling me into the elevator and shoving me against the elevator wall. I yelp, wincing at the pain that erupts throughout my back.

Then suddenly, his hand is around my throat, and he's choking me. I wrap my hands around his forearm, trying to pull him off me, but he's too strong.

"What do you want?" I manage to choke out.

"Your life," he simply says.

My life? Why? What did I ever do? Then I remember what Alessandro said. As his partner, my life will be in danger from his enemies. But he promised to protect me. Now where is he?

"Who . . . who do you work for?"

Despite not being able to see his face, I can tell that he's smiling. He leans forward until his mouth is by my ear.

"Gio Romano."

I gasp. Gio Romano.

Alessandro's father.

"Now, you will end things with Alessandro. If you want to live," he says. I shake my head. I promised Alessandro this wouldn't be too much for me. I promised him I'd never leave him. Not now that we've become one. "You might mistake your stupidity to be bravery, but I don't."

"I will never . . . leave him," I promise.

"Too bad," he says, and then his grip around my throat tightens to the point that I can't breathe. I tap his forearm, my eyes begging him to let me go, to spare me, but he's relentless. "You will die today."

His words, it's a promise. Just like mine was.

Shaking my head, I struggle against his grip. I don't want to die. I just found a reason to live. I can't. Not now.

Tears stream down my face.

Alessandro . . .

I'm sorry.

But just as my lids become heavy, the man is ripped off me. I gasp for breath, collapsing onto the floor. A gunshot rings in my head, and I flinch, covering my ears with my hands.

Someone rushes to me, placing their hands on my shoulders. I look up, surprised to see that we're now on the ground floor of the building. I didn't even feel the elevator move. Then my gaze finds the body lying on the floor in a pool of blood.

"Havyn," the person who saved me whispers, but all I can do is stare at the man who tried to kill me and who's now dead, with a gunshot wound to the head. "Havyn."

My head snaps to my saviour at the sound of how stern his voice is. My eyes meet a pair of pale blue ones, friendly blue eyes clouded with worry. He looks familiar. Where did I see him before?

"Are you okay?" he asks. Eyebrows furrowing, I think.

"Who are you?" I breathe out. "Why did you save me?"

"Alessandro sent me to look out for you now that he's back at work," he informs me.

"You still haven't told me who you are," I say.

Then he smiles, teeth and all. "My name is Luciano Romano."

Luciano Romano . . . Romano. Alessandro's brother.

Immediately, I flinch away. His father . . . their father sent someone to kill me.

"Hey. Hey," he calls out, his voice surprisingly gentle. "I'm not here to hurt you. In fact, I killed that man to *save* you."

"But your father . . ." I trail off.

"Look, things are very complicated at the moment, but we should return to the penthouse for now," he tells me.

I hesitantly nod, letting him help me up to my feet.

Luciano presses the button and the elevator takes us back up to the penthouse. He leads me inside and to the couch, then brings me a glass of water to calm me down, which I gratefully take. My throat feels so dry right now.

He sits down opposite me.

"What . . . what's happening?" I ask him.

He sighs. "Gio Romano . . . my father . . . he found out about you," he says.

"How?"

"About a week ago, Alessandro refused to marry the person my father had chosen for him. This really pissed our father off, so he set out to find out exactly why. I didn't tell him about you. I swear. But somehow, he found out. He was surprisingly quiet for a few days, and I knew that he was planning something, so I warned Alessandro. That's why he sent me to look out for you now that he's busy with the business affairs again," he explains.

So the man I'm with . . . when Alessandro told me his father would never accept me, I never thought it meant that he'd ever want to kill me. This . . . this is wrong on so many levels.

"But you don't need to worry. Alessandro will fix everything," he assures me, but at what cost? At what cost will he fix things.

My life is on the line right now. And even though I promised I'd never leave him, I can't help but wonder.

Is it really worth it?

No, Havyn. Don't think like that. Of course it's worth it.

Alessandro *is* worth it.

"Look, I know you're rattled by what just happened, scared even, but I have a request," he says, rubbing the back of his neck awkwardly.

"What is it?" I ask.

"Can you just not leave my brother?"

My eyes widen. How did he know . . .

"I know he's a lot of work, and I know that as an outsider, suddenly coming into this world, the mafia world . . . it's a lot. But please. My brother really cares for you. He's never *ever* asked me or Dante for help to protect a woman. You're really special to him, so I just hope that you appreciate that," he explains.

"I do," I tell him. "It's just . . . hard. I've lived my life on the edge, living in dangerous places with gangs, but none of them ever tried to actually kill me, and the fact that it's your father . . . *Alessandro's* father, I can't help how I feel."

He nods thoughtfully,

"I don't want to leave him. I-I love him." I admit for the first time ever. Luciano's eyes widen at my admission.

"Then we'll protect you," he says. "Not just Alessandro, but me, too. We'll protect you, and together, not even our father stands a chance."

"Thank you." I find myself sniffling.

He smiles. "You make my brother happy. I'll never let anyone take that away from him," he says, his words a promise.

I nod.

Then suddenly, Alessandro bursts in through the elevator doors, his eyes wide with worry.

"*Amore mio,*" he says with a whimper in relief upon seeing me. Then he collapses onto the couch next to me. "I'm so glad you're okay."

He pulls me into his arms, letting me rest my head on his shoulder, and finally, it's like the switch has been turned off, and I start to cry.

"I was so scared!" I cry out, gripping his shirt in between my fingers. "I thought I was going to die."

"I know, my love," he murmurs into my hair. "But I'd never let that happen."

He pulls away so he can look at me.

"You know that, right?"

I nod. He turns to Luciano.

"Thank you so much for saving her."

Luciano nods.

"Of course," he says.

"You know what we have to do, right?" Alessandro suddenly says. Luciano hesitantly nods.

"What you told me about before?" he asks, making sure, and Alessandro nods.

"What is it? What are you going to do?" I ask Alessandro. He turns back to me with a reassuring smile.

"It's okay. You don't have to worry about it."

"But I do," I insist, but he shakes his head. I look to Luciano, but he shakes his head, as well.

Sighing, I glare at Alessandro. "You promised me now that we're together, you'd never hide anything from me, even about your work," I tell him, my voice stern and accusatory.

"I'm not keeping anything from you, my love," he promises. "Besides, you'll be coming with us, so you'll find out then."

I reluctantly nod, and he breathes out a breath of relief that I'm letting it go.

Then his eyes darken as they land on my throat.

"He did this to you?" His voice sounds deadly. I nod. "I'll never forgive him. Gio Romano . . . I'll never forgive him."

"Alessandro, he's your father," I remind him, but he shakes his head.

"I don't care. He's dead to me."

I look at Luciano with pleading eyes. I don't want to be the cause of the destruction of Alessandro's relationship with his father. I, of all people, know the importance of family, having lost all of mine.

Luciano just shakes his head — admitting to me that he can't convince Alessandro to change his mind.

"Alessandro . . ."

"It's okay," he tells me. "Everything will be okay."

He places a soft kiss on my forehead before pulling me back into his arms. I sigh in the contentment of feeling him around me, but I can't help the worry that plagues my mind.

Just what's he planning to do now?

CHAPTER THIRTY-TWO: ALESSANDRO

A few days earlier

"Brother."

Luciano greets me with a grin, but it falls when he sees the expression on my face. He thinks I invited him over to my office for a friendly chat, but this is anything but that. This is serious.

After he called me the other day to tell me about our father finding out about Havyn, I've been on edge. He's been quiet, but I know better than to think he's maybe accepted my decision. It only means that when he decides to act, it's going to be very bad.

"What's happened?" he immediately asks, sinking into the chair.

"I need a favour," I say.

"Of course," he easily agrees. "What is it?"

"I need you to look over Havyn for me," I say. His eyebrows furrow.

"Aren't you looking after her?" he asks.

"I am, but I can't be around her all the time. I have to work, too. Which leaves her in danger while I'm gone," I tell him. "Father knows where I live, so that's a problem."

"Why not just move her someplace else?" he suggests.

I shake my head. "She'll ask why, and I don't want her knowing about this. Not yet," I say.

He nods. "I understand. And I'll watch over her," he agrees.

"Thank you." I truly am thankful to him. Other than Eddie, he's the only other person I can count on, especially when it comes to Havyn.

"It's not like I have anything better to do." He shrugs, but I'm still thankful. He's always been a dependable younger brother, more dependable than our eldest, Dante.

"And don't tell Dante about any of this," I warn him. He immediately nods.

"But . . . what if something does happen?" he questions, his tone becoming serious. "I can protect Havyn, but this is our father we're talking about."

I know what he means, and that's why I've come to a decision. "I really don't want to do this, but if he forces my hand, I'll have no choice."

"What is it?" he asks.

I look at him. "I'll step down."

"No!" he immediately exclaims. "If you step down, the title will automatically go to Dante. You know how bad that will be."

"I'm sorry, Luciano. I truly am, but Havyn comes first now," I say.

He sighs, slumping in his seat.

"Fuck."

I feel bad about springing this on him like this, but I can't help it.

I don't have any other choice.

Present day

I grip Havyn's hand in mine.

It's trembling. She's nervous.

Luciano glances at me through the mirror, but I look away. I need to focus solely on my love right now. I know that this is all very overwhelming for her. I can only imagine how she must be feeling right now. She's completely new to this. She's new to this world, *my* world. She barely got an introduction . . . no, she didn't get any introduction to my line of work before her life was threatened and almost taken away.

I don't know what I would have done without Luciano. If he wasn't there . . . Havyn wouldn't be alive right now.

I clench my free hand into a fist. The thought of losing her haunts me. The image of her bruised throat has scarred me. Never again will this happen. I won't let it.

We pull up in front of the Romano family house. We all used to live here together with our father, but I've long since moved out after I became Don. It was also a way for me to get out of Father's clutches.

But Luciano and Dante still stay here. Luciano mentioned moving out but said that he finds it too convenient living here, so he stays. And Dante . . . he's loyal to our father, to the bone, despite being betrayed by him. It's because he's hoping that one day, our father will change his mind and eventually give him the title of Don. Although I have a feeling his dream is about to come true today. All thanks to me and my sacrifice.

"Where are we?" *Amore mio*'s soft voice enters my ears.

"Our family home," Luciano answers for me. She tenses up.

"My love," I call out. "I know my father is in there, and you're scared, but he won't hurt you. Not with me there."

"I'm there, too," Luciano adds. She nods, squeezing my hand.

We walk into the house, and luckily for us, we don't have to go looking for our father because he's already sitting in the living room. With Dante. *Great.*

"Hi, Papa," Luciano greets, catching both of their attention. Father's eyes darken when he sees Havyn by my side, and she instinctively cowers, pressing herself into my side. I growl, glaring at him. How dare he intimidate her?

"So this must be the girl," Dante suddenly speaks up and stands, our father following after him. "The one who's stolen my poor younger brother's heart."

"How dare you bring her here," Father snaps.

"You tried to have her killed," I growl, my glare fierce.

"She's trying to ruin everything," he accuses.

"Shut up!" I snap. "The only one ruining things is you, *Papa*."

"How dare you? I'm your father!"

"I don't care!" I yell out. "The moment you tried to take the woman I love's life, you became dead to me."

Havyn freezes against me. *Fuck*. This is not how I wanted to tell her I love her for the first time.

"She'll never survive in our world, you know," Dante speaks up again, his expression blank. "She's too weak."

Luciano looks at me. That's my cue.

"And that's why I'm leaving our world."

Both his and Father's eyes widen.

"What are you saying?" Father questions.

Standing upright, I declare, "I'm stepping down."

Dante's lips curl up into a smirk while Father completely loses it.

"Are you insane?" he exclaims. "Why would you step down? You worked so hard to build the empire into what it is today, and now you're giving it all up? All for a girl?"

Havyn looks up at me with wide eyes.

"Yes, because I realised that there are more important things in life," I tell him.

"You're crazy." Father shakes his head.

"Maybe you're right. Maybe I am crazy. But this is my decision, and if it's the wrong one, I'll live with the consequences."

Luciano stares at me with a proud smile on his lips.

"Alessandro," my love whispers.

"I told you everything would be okay," I tell her, looking down at her.

"Are you sure about your decision?" Father asks, and I nod. Then I look to Dante.

"Dante, the position you've always dreamed about, it's yours now," I tell him, and he smirks. "But I have a request in exchange for all of this."

"What is it?" he asks.

"Ultimate protection. I don't care about myself. I can take care of myself. But this is for her, my love," I tell him.

"You wouldn't . . ." Father warns him. His control over us, over Dante, is slipping, and he's seeing it happen before his own eyes. Dante scoffs at Father before looking at me.

"Sure," he agrees. "Nothing will happen to your girl. You have my word."

If there's one good thing about Dante, it's that he always keeps his word, so I nod.

"Dante!" Father explodes.

"Oh, shut up," Dante boredly snaps. "You're loud."

Father's eyes widen, but he goes quiet. He realises now what's happened. Now that Dante is Don, the whole loyal puppy façade has faded, leaving behind the true Dante. And Father has no control over this Dante. He knows this better than anyone else.

"Yay!" Luciano suddenly cheers. "It all worked out!"

I chuckle, staring at my ball-of-sunshine younger brother.

Havyn wraps her arms around me, snuggling her face into me.

"Thank you," she says. It's two simple words that's nothing compared to what I've just given up for her, but the raw emotion in her voice makes it all worth it. Fuck, I love this girl.

She looks up at me with determined eyes. Then suddenly, "I'll love you forever."

My eyes to widen in surprise.

"I promise."

I smile, pulling her into my arms. "That's all I need from you, *Amore mio.*"

Luciano stares at the two of us with slightly glassy eyes, the sadness in his eyes evident. I know what he's thinking about. *Who* he's thinking about.

Then he snaps out of it.

"I have to go," he announces, sending me a look, and I nod. *Go to her, Luciano.*

And then he's gone.

"Well, Father, looks like someone new is in charge," Dante smugly says.

"Dante . . . my son." Father is panicky. He knows he's done Dante wrong over the years, and finally, Dante can get back at him for all of that.

"Dante," I call out, catching his attention. "Go easy on the poor man. He's nearly dead, you know."

He chuckles, saluting me. This is the heartiest moment I've ever had with Dante, and it's quite refreshing. I hope now that he's Don, he'll go back to who he was before.

"Come on, *amore mio*," I say. "Let's go home."

Home. Finally I can call it that. Because she's there.

EPILOGUE: ALESSANDRO

"Fuck!"

I pound into her, my thrusts relentless and quickening with each one. She moans underneath me, her back arching.

Sweat coats both our bodies, our skin sticking together. Fuck, I love fucking her. I've fucked many women in my life, but none of them get me like she does. So out of control. So animalistic. So needy. So fucking hard.

When she comes, she clenches around me, sending me into an oblivion of pleasure that has me teetering off the edge, and I release myself inside her for the millionth time ever.

Collapsing next to her, I pull her into my arms. She breathes out in satisfaction. I can't help but reach down, grabbing her left hand in mine. The diamond on her ring finger shines in the light. She looks at it, too, her lips forming a smile.

I can still barely believe it. After being alone for so long, I've finally found her, my soulmate. My everything. And now we're engaged.

"I love you," I can't help myself but tell her.

She smiles. "I love you, too."

I'll never get tired of hearing her say that. Those three words. Three simple words that have me melting completely.

Leaning down, I dig my hand into her messy hair and press my lips to hers. She rolls over so that she's on top of me, and it has me hard within seconds. I should be embarrassed by how sensitive I am and how quickly I get hard, but I'm not. In fact, I quite like showing her. Because that way, she can see how much she affects me. How much I truly want her.

"You think you can give me another orgasm?" she murmurs against my lips, and I smile, recalling the moment I said those very words to her. So I nod, and she smiles before sliding down onto me. I groan, gripping her hips.

We make love this time, and about three more times before we are both completely spent. I was lucky to meet and fall in love with someone who matches my sexual stamina. This girl can go on for hours on end, and that's another thing I love about her. That, and the fact that she never says no to me.

"No."

Luciano blinks at my fiancée, shocked. "But —"

"I said no," she insists.

I chuckle, shaking my head at the two of them.

"We're not having a big wedding. We're getting married at city hall."

The fact that my brother is the one insisting on a big wedding while my love just wants to get married at city hall has to be the most comical thing ever.

"I don't understand why you don't want a big wedding. It's a Romano wedding. We're Romano's. We do big," he persists, but she shakes her head.

"I don't care. I want to get married at city hall, and that's that." She gives her final say, and he nods in defeat.

"Hey, when you get married to Caterina, you can have as big a wedding as you want," I tell him when I see how truly disappointed he is by this.

"It's not that," he says, completely skipping over me talking about Caterina. "Of course I'll have a big wedding. It's just . . . you're my brother, and I wanted to see you walk down the aisle. I wanted to give a speech and everything. I wanted the whole shebang."

"You do realise the bride walks down the aisle and not the groom, right?" my love points out, but he ignores her.

"I mean, when will I get a chance to witness another brother get married?" he whines.

"There's still Dante," Havyn feels the need to point out.

"Oh, please," he scoffs. "That guy will never get married."

Havyn leans back on the couch.

"If you want, you can come to the city hall with us and watch us get married. You can even say your speech," she offers, and he lights up, nodding.

"Then it's settled," I announce. Finally, everyone's happy. Honestly, I have no thoughts about this. I don't care whether we have a big wedding or get married at city hall. As long as at the end of the day, I can call her my wife.

Now that the argument is over, Havyn and Luciano go on as usual, their conversation filled with smiles and giggles. He's the only man I feel comfortable having around Havyn. I trust him, and it helps that he already has eyes for someone else.

When Luciano finally leaves, my love and I snuggle up in bed.

"You happy?" I can't help but ask her. After everything she's been through because of me, I have to be sure.

"Of course I am," she says, luckily not picking up on my nervousness concerning this. "Are you?"

I nod with a smile before leaning down and kissing her.

I couldn't be happier.

ABOUT THE AUTHOR

I have lived my entire life Cape Town, South Africa where my life is run by 2 furbabies, a husky named Saskya, and a cat named Stripey. I'm a hopeless romantic who dreams of having the kind of love I read and write in books. Coffee and music are my writing companions. When not writing, I like creating art with my hands and paint tiny canvases. My sister has never let me live down THE oven incident. In my own defence, she asked me to turn the oven on, she did not ask me to set the temperature. My only secret, my obsessions are known by those who know me best, but even they don't know about my solo karaoke sessions.

www.ingramcontent.com/pod-product-compliance
Lightning Source LLC
Chambersburg PA
CBHW060817120626
46557CB00001B/259